MITCH
AND
AMY

OTHER YEARLING BOOKS YOU WILL ENJOY:

Socks, BEVERLY CLEARY

Henry and the Paper Route, BEVERLY CLEARY

Otis Spofford, BEVERLY CLEARY

The Mouse and the Motorcycle, BEVERLY CLEARY

Emily's Runaway Imagination, BEVERLY CLEARY

Henry and Ribsy, BEVERLY CLEARY

Beezus and Ramona, BEVERLY CLEARY

Ellen Tebbits, BEVERLY CLEARY

Henry and the Clubhouse, BEVERLY CLEARY

Henry Huggins, BEVERLY CLEARY

YEARLING BOOKS are designed especially to entertain and enlighten young people. Charles F. Reasoner, Professor Emeritus of Children's Literature and Reading, New York University, is consultant to this series.

For a complete listing of all Yearling titles, write to Dell Publishing Co., Inc., Promotion Department, P.O. Box 3000, Pine Brook, N.J. 07058.

MITCH AND AMY

BEVERLY CLEARY

illustrated by George Porter

A YEARLING BOOK

Published by
Dell Publishing Co., Inc.
1 Dag Hammarskjold Plaza
New York, New York 10017

Yearling ® TM 913705, Dell Publishing Co., Inc.

ISBN: 0-440-45411-5

Reprinted by arrangement with William Morrow & Company, Inc.
Printed in the United States of America
Sixth Dell printing—October 1983
CW

CONTENTS

MITCH
AND
AMY

1

MITCHELL'S SKATE BOARD

MITCHELL HUFF's day began like any other summer day—with a squabble with his twin sister Amy. At breakfast Amy grabbed a cereal box top and said, "I'm going to send away for the plastic harmonica that looks like an ear of corn."

"Oh, no you don't!" said Mitchell. "It's my turn to get the box top."

"It is not!" said Amy. "You got the last one."

"But it wasn't a good box top," said Mitchell. "How come you get all the good box tops?"

"I don't," said Amy. "You sent away for the pedometer."

"Yes, but it broke the first time I used it," said Mitchell.

"That wasn't my fault," said Amy.

"It's no fair," said Mitchell. "You always grab the good box tops, and then don't send away for things."

"Be quiet, both of you," said Mrs. Huff, "or I shall serve hot oatmeal every morning, three hundred sixty-five days of the year, and you won't have any box tops to send away."

Mr. Huff, who had to catch a bus to the city, glanced at his watch and said, "That ought to settle this morning's squabble."

"Okay, Mom. You win," Mitchell said amiably.

"Oatmeal, ick," said Amy.

After breakfast Mitchell went out to the patio to work on the skate board he was building out of an old board and a roller skate while Amy went to her room and began to play her cello. That's funny, thought Mitchell, sawing the board in two, nobody told her to practice. There was something familiar about the catchy tune his sister was playing, and Mitchell grinned when he recognized that it was not her lesson, but the music from a television commercial. That Amy!

In a few minutes the cello was silent, but Amy's tune ran through Mitchell's head half the morning. He was pounding the last nail around the half of the skate fastened to the front of the board when Amy came out the back door.

"I thought I heard Marla come through the gate," Amy said. She picked a dandelion that had gone to seed in a flower bed and held it up to examine it more closely.

Mitchell gave the nail a final bang with the hammer and sat back on his heels, waiting for Amy to say something about his skate board, but Amy was looking at the ball of dandelion fluff as if she found it a thing of magic and, while Mitchell watched, she closed her eyes to make a wish.

Mitchell looked at his sister standing there in her playclothes with her knees bruised, her brown hair falling to her shoulders, and her summer freckles bright in the September sunshine. Her lips were puckered beside the dandelion's white head as if they had been drawn up by a string. He saw her chest rise as she drew a deep breath and held it for a moment.

Suddenly the temptation was too great for Mitchell. Gathering his breath he rose and moved

swiftly and silently across the concrete on his rubber soles.

Whoof! Mitchell blew as hard as he could and sent every one of Amy's dandelion seeds dancing off into the sunshine.

Amy's eyes flew open, and for a moment she stared at the empty stem in her hand. Then with a yell of rage she flung it onto the patio. "Mitchell Huff!" she shrieked. "You spoiled my wish! I'll get you for this!" There was nothing dreamy about Amy as she began to chase Mitchell. Around and around the patio they went, sneakers pounding up on the bench and down on the concrete again, Mitchell ducking and sidestepping Amy and always managing to stay just out of her grasp.

"You're despicable!" cried Amy, who already read on the fifth-grade level or even higher, although she was about to enter the fourth grade. Mitchell felt his sister's fingers on his shirt and jerked away. Around and around they went, and as they grew short of breath they both began to laugh.

Mrs. Huff opened the back door and stepped into the patio with a jar of peanut butter and a knife in her hand. "You two," she said. "Stop it."

The chase slowed and came to a halt. "He blew
—the fluff off—my dandelion—when I was about
to—make a wish," said Amy, giggling and gasping
and appealing for justice.

"I couldn't—help it," panted Mitchell. "She was
just—standing there—all puckered up with her eyes
closed and suddenly something came over me—"

"Something comes over you altogether too
often." Mrs. Huff spread a gob of peanut butter
on a pinecone tied to the branch of a crab-apple
tree outside the dining-room window. "I saw the
first chickadees of the season this morning, and I
thought if I started putting peanut butter out again
we might persuade them to stay with us for the
winter. Amy, pick another dandelion, and I'll
stand guard while you make your wish."

"It won't be the same," said Amy, but she found
a second dandelion.

"Mitch, if you blow the fluff off Amy's dandelion this time, I'll spread you with peanut butter
and leave you for the chickadees," said Mrs. Huff,
as she smeared peanut butter between the scales of
the pinecone. Since Amy had made a bird feeder
out of the pinecone for a Brownie project in the

third grade, Mrs. Huff had become interested in bird watching. "Mom's feathered friends" her children called the juncoes, sparrows, and chickadees that grew fat on her peanut butter.

"I'll try to control myself," said Mitchell, when his mother had finished with the pinecone. "It will be a struggle, but I'll try." He noticed that this time Amy did not shut her eyes; she remained vigilant until with one breath she had sent all the dandelion seeds flying out across the patio. "What did you wish?" he asked.

"As if I would tell you," said Amy.

Mrs. Huff screwed the lid back onto the peanut-butter jar. "I know what I wish. I wish you two would stop bickering. I'll be glad when school starts."

"Mom! You said a bad word," said Mitchell. "It begins with s." He was about to try standing on his skate board when Marla Brodsky came through the patio gate.

"Hi, Amy. Hello, Mrs. Huff." Marla stopped when she saw what Mitchell had been working on. "How come you built a skate board when you already have a skate board?" she asked.

"I just wanted to, is all," answered Mitchell.

"I know," said Marla. "I like to make things, too."

Mitchell already knew she did. Marla and Amy were always making things when they were not pretending something. He stepped carefully onto his skate board and hoped it would bear his weight. Bending nails around the skate halves had not been easy. Nothing cracked and nothing fell off. He bounced to test the strength of his skate board, and still it held. It was sturdy enough to hold a sixty-seven-pound boy.

"It looks like a fine job to me," said Mrs. Huff. Mitchell felt this comment was generous of his mother, who thought all skate boards were dangerous.

"Do you suppose it will really work?" Amy asked.

Mitchell stepped off his board and picked it up. "I think I'll go road test it. So long, Mom."

"You mean sidewalk test it," answered his mother. "You stay out of the street with that thing."

"Sure, Mom." Mitchell knew his mother was nervous, because all the streets in their neighborhood were hilly and winding and only a few had sidewalks.

"And please don't break your neck," said Mrs. Huff, "and don't run down any little old ladies."

"You can count on me, Mom."

Mitchell carried his homemade skate board through the patio gate, down the steep driveway to a gently sloping street with a sidewalk. Mitchell felt good. It was a bright, clear day. Down below he could see the red tile roofs of the University, and across the bay he could see San Francisco and the Golden Gate Bridge. He had built himself a skate board that was probably going to work, and in a few days he and Amy would go into the fourth grade. Why shouldn't he feel good? He had everything to feel good about. He set his skate board on the sidewalk, stepped onto it, and began to coast slowly down the sloping concrete.

"Yea!" Mitchell cheered out loud. The skate board he had built himself really did work! Of course, it did not steer easily like the skate board he had saved his allowance for, but it worked and that was the important thing. Not often did something that Mitchell had built really work. His sister Amy was different. She was always making something that worked—a crocheted pot holder or a bird feeder out of a pinecone—but Mitchell doubted if even she could build a working skate board.

The sidewalk curved, and although Mitchell tried steering by shifting his weight, the skate board headed for the street. He jumped off and caught the board before it coasted off the curb. Around the curve he set it on the sidewalk once more, and feeling pleased with himself, his skate board, and the sunny day, he coasted on down the sidewalk past a small boy who was sitting out in front of his house on his tricycle.

"Hi there, Johnny," said Mitchell, as he coasted by.

"Why don't you thut up?" said Johnny.

"Okay, Johnny." Mitchell knew Johnny was wishing he was old enough to have a skate board, and Mitchell wished Johnny were too. His neighborhood was full of little boys and teen-age boys, girls of all ages, but no nine-year-old boys. Next Mitchell had to stop for a lady who was backing out of her driveway. "Did you build that yourself?" she asked.

"Yes, I did," said Mitchell modestly.

"Well, you did a fine job," said the lady, as she backed out into the street, "but be careful you don't break your neck."

Mitchell coasted to the end of the slope in the sidewalk, and on his way he met the mailman, a milkman, and a lady who was setting a sprinkler on her lawn. They all told him to be careful not to break his neck, but this attitude did not surprise Mitchell. All grown-ups expected all boys on skate boards to break their neck. When he came to the level part of the sidewalk, he picked up his skate board, walked back up the slope, and started all over again.

"Hi there, Johnny," he said, coasting toward the little boy on the tricycle once more.

Johnny took two fingers out of his mouth. "You thut up," he said.

Mitchell grinned and coasted along, holding his arms out for balance. He felt good to be so much older than Johnny on his tricycle, to be old enough to ride on a skate board he had built himself. Mitchell felt so good he decided he might even use his other skate to build a skate board for his sister.

Amy had really been pretty good lately, and she hadn't tattled when he helped himself to more than his share of the cookies she had baked. Of course, Amy had been mad a little while ago, but he couldn't say he blamed her. He knew he shouldn't tease his sister so much, but he couldn't seem to help himself. He would think he wasn't going to tease her, and then he would see her doing something like making a wish on that dandelion and something just seemed to come over him. . . .

The funny part was, although he wouldn't want Amy to know, Mitchell liked being known as one of the Huff twins. "Mitchell Huff?" people would say the first time they met him. "You must be one of the Huff twins," as if being a twin was something special. And Mitchell felt that being a twin was something special. Special but sometimes difficult.

The sound of skate boards approaching behind him interrupted Mitchell's thoughts. Boys! Someone to play with! He jumped off his own board beside the bus-stop sign, turned, and saw two boys, both of whom he recognized, coasting toward him in the street. The older boy, Dwight Hill, usually called Dwight Pill, was going to start junior high school and had been famous at Bay View

School, when he was in the sixth grade, because he was the first person to bring a battery-powered eraser to school. Mitchell was not surprised to see him riding the longest, most expensive skate board manufactured.

The second boy, Alan Hibbler, was riding a medium-priced skate board. Alan was a good-looking boy who was about to enter the fifth grade and who was the son of a famous scientist at the University. The whole school knew about Alan's father, Judson Hibbler, who was so famous that his picture had been in *Life* magazine.

The two boys coasted to a stop at the curb beside Mitchell. "Hi there, kid," said Alan.

"Hi." Mitchell did not much care to be called *kid* by a boy who was only one grade ahead of him in school.

"Look at his little skate board," scoffed Dwight, who was noted not only for his battery-powered eraser, but for the number of times he had been sent to the principal's office.

"Did you build it all by yourself?" Alan wanted to know. Mitchell could see he was trying to act big because he was with a junior-high-school boy.

"I have a boughten one at home," said Mitchell,

indignant at the way he was being treated. "I just wanted to see if I could make one that would work."

"I bet," said Alan.

Mitchell's stomach suddenly tightened as if it were clenched into a fist. "Well, I do have a real one at home," he said defiantly.

No one spoke for a moment. Dwight pulled a cigarette out of his shirt pocket, tapped it on his wrist, and stuck one end into his mouth.

Mitchell watched, fascinated. "You're not old enough to smoke," he said.

"Who says so?" Dwight squinted as he struck a match and held it to his cigarette.

"Yes, who says so?" echoed Alan.

Mitchell did not answer. If Dwight was stupid enough to smoke, that was his business. Mitchell only wished he would go someplace else to do it and stop spoiling his fun.

Dwight flicked out the match and took a deep puff on the cigarette. Mitchell could not help watching while Dwight's face grew red, his eyes watered, he spluttered, and was finally forced to give in to an embarrassing fit of coughing.

Mitchell managed not to laugh out loud, but he

could not keep the corners of his mouth from quirking. Old Dwight wasn't as big as he thought he was. One puff and he was practically choking to death. Another puff would probably make him sick, but after all that gasping and coughing he wouldn't dare try a second puff.

"What's so funny?" demanded Alan, embarrassed and angry because the boy he had been imitating looked ridiculous.

"Old Dwight," said Mitchell. "That's what's funny."

Dwight struggled for breath, which seemed to make Alan madder. Before Mitchell realized what the other boy was doing, Alan had picked up the homemade skate board and was pounding it with all his strength against the bus-stop sign. There was a sound of splintering wood and another fit of coughing from Dwight.

"You cut that out!" yelled Mitchell, making a lunge for Alan. He did not care if Alan was bigger. He was not going to get away with wrecking the skate board Mitchell had worked so hard to build. His fingers clutched at Alan's T-shirt.

Alan shook him off. The skate board split and one of the skate halves fell to the sidewalk. Before

Mitchell could get his hands on the skate, Alan had it and was beating it on the concrete until it was bent and twisted out of shape. Then Alan turned on Mitchell with menace on his face. "Start running," he ordered.

Furious, Mitchell faced the two older boys with his fists clenched. Who did they think they were, pounding up his skate that way and then giving him orders?

"You heard him," said Dwight, finally able to speak. "Start running."

Mitchell did not move, and the two boys stepped forward. "Now," said Alan. "*N-o-w.* Now."

A lot of thoughts seethed through Mitchell's mind—he did not like to be spelled at. Alan and Dwight weren't fair. They had no right to gang up on him this way. They were two against one, and both boys were bigger. Mitchell realized there was only one decision he could make and that he had to make it now. He turned and ran.

The bent skate half came flying past. The splintered board with the other half skate still attached to it hit Mitchell's back. Mitchell paused long enough to scoop up the remains of his skate board before he ran up the hill toward home. He twisted his ankle on the gravel at the edge of the road where the sidewalk ended and behind him he could hear the boys laughing.

Mitchell held back tears of humiliation, but he could not keep his heart from pounding with exertion and fury. Let them laugh. They were just a couple of no-good bullies. Who did they think they were anyway, a couple of characters on some TV program? Well, they weren't. They were plain old boys even if one did go to junior high and the other had a famous father. Mitchell stopped running and dragged himself on up the hill, lugging his broken skate board. His back hurt where the board had hit him, and he felt hot and sweaty as he plodded up his steep driveway. Hot, sweaty, and defeated. His day was spoiled. His whole school year was spoiled. Dwight would be going down the hill to junior high school, but Mitchell would have to see Alan every day at school, sometimes even on the way to school, and he would always know, and Alan would always know, that Mitchell had turned and run.

The knowledge that running was the only thing he could have done did not help Mitchell much.

I'll get Alan for this, he thought, but he did not really believe what he was thinking. Alan was older and Alan was bigger. There was not much Mitchell could do to him.

Mitchell paused for breath and looked up the driveway at his redwood and glass house under the eucalyptus trees. He tried to catch sight of Amy and Marla, but the big windows only gave back the reflection of blue sky and eucalyptus leaves turning and fluttering in the breeze. He hoped the girls had gone to Marla's house to play, because he did not want them to see him come dragging home with his broken skate board in his hands.

2

AMY'S THIRD DANDELION

AMY had not made a real wish at all. When Mitchell had blown away her first wish, she had been standing with her eyes closed trying to decide which of several wishes to choose—something with whipped cream on it for dessert, lots of birthday-party invitations in the fourth grade, or the president of the United States abolishing the multiplication tables.

On the second dandelion Amy had simply wished that Mitchell would not blow off the dandelion fluff before she blew it off herself, and this wish she felt did not count.

"What are you going to wear the first day of school?" asked Marla Brodsky. "If it isn't too hot, I'm going to wear my new pleated skirt."

"Me too," agreed Amy. "Mom says it is too long, but I like it that way. It makes me feel like a ten-year-old."

"Are you and Mitch going to be in the same class in the fourth grade?" Marla asked, as the two girls went into the house.

"They won't let us," answered Amy. "They say twins should be separated. We haven't been in the same class since kindergarten." By "they" Amy meant parents, teachers, and Mr. Greer, the principal.

"Aren't you glad?" Marla asked. "I wouldn't want to be in the same class with my brother if I had a brother."

"Um . . . not exactly, I guess. It's sort of fun to have people talk about the Huff twins." And it was, but there was another side to being a twin that Amy sometimes thought about when she and Mitchell had a fight. As long as she could remember her brother had always been there sharing birthdays and parents and all the important things. While Amy would much rather be a twin than not be a twin, still, there were times when she wished she could have everything to herself for a little while without feeling she had to keep ahead of her brother.

"It's funny, I used to think twins would be alike," remarked Marla. "You and Mitch are so different. You're always reading, and Mitch is always running and jumping around."

"That's because we're not identical," Amy explained, leading the way into her untidy room. She had put her cello under her bed where no one could step on it and where her mother would not see it and remind her to practice, but her desk and dresser were cluttered with sewing things, stuffed animals, books, crayons, and parts of a doll's blue-willow tea set. The floor was strewn with bright snips of origami paper, a crumpled drawing, and one dirty sock, which Amy now shoved under the bed with her foot.

"You're lucky," said Marla. "My mother makes me pick up my room every single day."

"My mother says she gets tired of nagging," said Amy. Mrs. Huff said Amy's room was as untidy as a mouse nest, but Amy was old enough to take care of it herself. Amy enjoyed the idea of living in a mouse nest and so the state of her room did not bother her. It only bothered her mother.

Marla went over to Amy's bulletin board to look at the calendar on which Amy always recorded important events. On the square for September first she had written "106 days to Christmas" in red. On September second, "Today I read a good book." September third was important because "We had Jello with whipped cream."

Out in the living room a man spoke in a calm, even voice. "Pages two hundred eleven to two hundred nineteen. Black-capped chickadee," he said.

"Who's that?" Marla asked, startled because Mrs. Huff had been alone when they entered the house.

"*Chick-a-dee-dee. Chick-a-dee-dee. Fee-bee. Fee-bee.*" A bird twittered in the living room.

"That's just Mom's birdcall records," explained Amy. "She's nearsighted for a bird watcher so she's trying to identify birds by learning their calls from phonograph records."

"Mountain chickadee," announced the man's voice.

"*Fee-fee-fee. Tsick-a-zee-zee,*" said the bird.

"It sounds as if there are real birds in the living room," said Marla.

"I know. That's what the cat next door thought at first," said Amy. "What shall we play?"

"Dress up," answered Marla promptly. "Let's pretend we're pioneers."

"Yes, let's," agreed Amy. Marla always wanted to do the right things at the right times. Some girls would have wanted to watch Mitchell road test his skate board, but not Marla. Marla liked to read old-fashioned stories about pioneer hardships, too, and she was always ready to pretend.

Amy opened the bottom drawer of her dresser, which was spilling over with dress-up clothes her mother had collected for her, a gleaming, shimmering jumble of satins, taffetas, velvets, and chiffons in rainbow colors.

Marla picked out a pink chiffon bridesmaid dress, looked at it critically, and asked, "Don't you have any old calico dresses? Pioneer girls didn't wear slithering things like this."

"Nobody has calico dresses anymore," Amy pointed out. "I'm not even sure what calico looks like."

"I know, but silks—" Marla's voice trailed off wistfully.

Out in the living room the man's voice spoke calmly, as if he had never been sad or angry in his life. "Curve-billed thrasher," he said.

A bird obediently answered, "*Whit-wheet! Whit-wheet!*"

Amy knew what Marla meant. The dresses that Mrs. Huff had saved or collected from friends or bought from the Goodwill for Amy were perfect for princesses but not for pioneers. "Oh well," said Amy. "Come on. We can pretend they are calico." If they were going to pretend, they might as well really pretend. "Dibs on being Laura."

"Okay," agreed Marla. "I'll be Mary." Laura and Mary were characters in the *Little House* stories, the girls' favorite books, about the pioneer adventures of Laura Ingalls and her family. Marla pawed through the pile of dress-up clothes and dragged out the plainest dress she could find, a pale blue chiffon evening gown. "Let's have hardships. Let's pretend there's a blizzard."

Amy pulled a raspberry-colored satin dress over her head and groped for the sleeves. "Zip me up the back," she said, when she found them. "And let's

pretend our father has gone to town to buy sup-
plies. That gets him out of the way."

Marla zipped up Amy's dress. "How will we
get rid of our mother?" The first rule in any game
of pretend was to get rid of parents as soon as
possible. Have them die of pneumonia, let Indians
shoot them with bows and arrows, but get rid of
them.

"She could go out into the blizzard to take care
of the animals—"

"No, that wouldn't really get rid of her," objected Marla. "She would tie a rope from the house
to the barn and follow it back so she wouldn't
lose her way. We'll have to think of something
else."

Amy thought a moment. How could they get
rid of their mother? "We could have her away
taking care of a sick neighbor, and we are all
alone in the house with the baby—" She picked up
her Pooh bear and wrapped it in a doll blanket.
"Here's the baby—"

"And let's make it that the snow is up to the
roof—"

"And blowing through the chinks—"

"And the wolves are howling outside—"

"And we are just about out of food—"

"There's nothing left but a little cornmeal—"

"Which we have to cook in the fireplace—the space under my desk can be the fireplace—"

"And the baby is crying—wah-wah, that's the baby crying."

"And let's make it that we are out of wood—"

"And have to chop up the chairs—"

"So we won't freeze to death—"

"What will we use for chairs?"

Amy thought a moment. What could they use for chairs? "I know! We can roll up newspapers and pretend they are pieces of broken-up chairs."

Marla nodded. "And we can hear the wolves coming closer—"

"And we are afraid Father is lost in the blizzard—"

"Or devoured by wolves—" Both girls ran out of breath and ideas at the same time.

In the living room the man on the record spoke in the even voice that sounded as if he had never hit his sister or yelled at a ball game, "Hermit thrush."

"*Tuk-tuk-tuk*," answered the hermit thrush.

"What about Indians?" asked Amy.

"Not in a blizzard," said Marla. "Just wolves."

Amy had another idea. "I think we should be wearing aprons. Pioneer girls were always wearing aprons. Clean ones. Come on, let's get some of Mom's."

Holding up their silken skirts so they wouldn't trip, Amy and her friend trailed into the living room where Mrs. Huff looked up from her *Field Guide to Western Birds*, which she was studying along with the record of birdcalls.

"We're going to borrow a couple of aprons," Amy explained. "We're playing we're pioneer girls enduring hardships."

"In those dresses?" Mrs. Huff looked amused.

"We're pretending they are calico," explained Amy. "They are all we have to dress up in. Nobody wears calico anymore."

"I see what you mean," said Mrs. Huff. "You could hardly be pioneer girls in your mother's old slacks."

"Come on, Marla, let's find the aprons." Amy pulled two aprons out of a drawer in the kitchen and handed one to Marla, who put it on over her chiffon evening gown, but somehow, now that they had left the bedroom and had spoken to Mrs.

Huff, the spell was broken. The game of pretend no longer seemed urgent. "I suppose we should cook something, especially since we're burning up the chairs," said Amy.

"Some cornmeal mush or something," agreed Marla.

"Maybe we could really cook something." Amy cooked at every opportunity and was particularly good at making French toast.

"Yes, let's cook something and pretend it's cornmeal mush." Marla was as enthusiastic about cooking as Amy, although her mother did not often permit her to make a mess in the kitchen.

The birdcall record had come to an end, and Mrs. Huff had overheard the conversation. "You may make some instant pudding if you like," she said. "There's a package in the cupboard with the canned goods. Lemon-flavored, I think, so it will at least be yellow like cornmeal mush."

"Thanks, Mom." Amy found the package of pudding mix and removed the plastic cover from the electric mixer, explaining, "I know pioneers didn't have one of these, but I love to use the mixer."

"So do I," agreed Marla.

Outside the kitchen door Amy heard the sound of a skate being thrown down on the concrete patio, and then she saw Mitchell, sweaty, red-faced, and cross, come through the back door. He glared at her and demanded, "How come you always get to use the electric mixer?"

Amy had not forgotten the dandelion fluff Mitchell had blown away before she could make a wish. "Because I'm a girl, that's why," she answered. "I bet you're cross because your old skate board wouldn't work. It probably fell apart the minute you started downhill."

"It did too work! It worked just fine." Mitchell was furious. He stood there with his fists clenched and one lock of hair, the one he never could slick down, standing straight up on the crown of his head. His shirttail was hanging out. Mitchell never could remember to tuck in the back of his shirt.

Amy knew that as much as her brother liked motors, his anger was not caused by her getting to use the electric mixer. Something had happened to Mitchell while he was road testing his skate board.

At that point Mrs. Huff came into the kitchen. "Why, Mitchell!" she exclaimed, seeing his red face and his scowl. "Whatever is the matter?"

"Nothing," said Mitchell ferociously. "Why is everybody picking on me?"

"Nobody is picking on you," said Mrs. Huff. "Something is the matter or you wouldn't be acting this way, but, if you don't want to tell us, you don't have to."

Amy saw anger drain out of Mitchell's face but hurt remain. Now she understood that something had hurt her brother's feelings and without even knowing what it was, she felt indignant. How dare anyone hurt Mitchell's feelings!

Marla, who was not even a member of the family, looked sympathetic too.

Mitchell kicked the leg of the kitchen table with the toe of his sneaker, and Amy noticed that their mother restrained herself from telling him not to kick the furniture. "Aw, a couple of guys—" he said and stopped.

"What did they do?" Mrs. Huff asked gently.

"They wrecked my skate board and pounded up my skate so it isn't any good anymore and told me to start running and then threw the pieces at me." Mitchell scowled at the floor when he had finished.

Amy was shocked. Mitchell's skate board that he had worked so hard to build! Oh, poor Mitchell—

"Why, Mitchell—what did you do?" asked Mrs. Huff, and Amy could see that her mother was just as shocked as she was.

Mitchell did not take his eyes from the floor. "I ran. What else could I do? There were two of them and they were older than me and bigger."

"Then you did the wise thing," said Mrs. Huff. "You would have been foolish to try to stay and fight."

"Do you really think so?" asked Mitchell, looking up at his mother.

"Yes, I do." Mrs. Huff was emphatic. "You will always find bullies in this world and the wisest thing to do is stay away from them. Who were these boys?"

"Alan Hibbler and Dwight Hill."

"Alan Hibbler. Isn't he the son of Judson Hibbler, the distinguished—" began Mrs. Huff.

Amy interrupted. "That old Alan Hibbler," she said scornfully. "He thinks he's so big because his father is famous. He used to kick my lunch box when I was in the second grade."

"He sure does think he's big," agreed Marla. "He grabbed my raincoat once when I was running and tore the pocket right out."

"And once when I was a Brownie he pulled off my beanie and threw it into the boys' bathroom," continued Amy. "I had to ask the custodian to get it back for me."

"Well, he is bigger than me," said Mitchell, "and he's the one who pounded up my skate."

"But he looks like such a nice boy," said Mrs. Huff. "He's clean-cut and has good manners."

"He's the type who's nice to grown-ups but not to children," Amy explained. "He doesn't have evil beady eyes or anything like that, but he's a bully just the same."

"I don't think a boy should be allowed to get away with destroying another boy's skate," said Mrs. Huff. "Perhaps I should telephone his—"

"Mom!" Mitchell was alarmed. "Promise you won't call his family!"

"But Mitchell, the boy destroyed your property."

Amy knew exactly how her brother felt. "No,

Mom, don't call," she pleaded, backing up Mitchell.

"He would really get me if you did that," said Mitchell. "Boy, he would really get me then."

Amy watched her mother study Mitchell's face. Please don't call, she thought. Please, please don't call. Mitchell was going to have enough trouble. If Alan Hibbler had made him run once, what was to keep him from trying again? And he would be sure to try if he thought Mitchell had got him in trouble with his family.

"I think Mitchell is right," said Marla timidly, because, after all, she was not a member of the family.

"Believe me, Mom. I know," insisted Mitchell. "Sometimes parents embarrass their children and get them into all sorts of trouble."

"Yes, Mitchell knows," Amy agreed earnestly. "Alan really would be after him." Although she and Mitchell no longer walked to school together, she knew her brother often met Alan on the way.

Mrs. Huff relented. "All right, Mitchell, I won't call. But I'm not sure it's good for Alan to let him get away with destroying your skate."

"Mitchell has outgrown roller skating anyway,"

said Amy, anxious lest her mother change her mind.

"That's not the point," said Mrs. Huff. "The point is, if Alan is allowed to get away with this, what will he try to do next?"

"Nothing, I hope," said Mitchell. "Just don't go calling his family. Maybe he'll forget the whole thing."

Amy could see that her mother was still troubled, and she was troubled herself. She did not like to think of Alan telling her brother to start running. The whole thing sounded like part of the kind of television program her mother would not let her watch. Alan seemed to think he was some kind of TV character, a bully on a shooting program. And the skate board! Thinking about the broken skate board her brother had worked so hard to build all by himself hurt Amy. Thinking how Mitchell was feeling hurt her too.

Amy no longer felt like pretending she was a pioneer girl enduring hardships, cooking cornmeal mush in a fireplace during a blizzard. The magic had gone out of the game, and she did not want to pretend anymore. She thought about Mitchell and how much he liked anything with a motor, and so she said, "Mitch, would you like to make the instant pudding?"

Mitchell looked suspicious, and Amy knew he was wondering why she was giving up a chance to use the electric mixer. "How come?" he asked.

"Oh well, if you don't want to—" Not for anything would Amy let her brother know how sorry she felt about what had happened.

"Sure I want to."

"Then go ahead." Now Amy knew what she wanted to wish for on her third dandelion. She would wish that that old bully, Alan Hibbler, would leave her brother alone. And when she made her wish she would blow so hard that every single dandelion seed would fly off dancing into the wind.

3

THE
QUARREL

"Do I really get to make the pudding?" Mitchell asked his mother after Marla had discovered it was time to go home.

"Of course," answered Mrs. Huff.

"And be sure you don't spoil it," said Amy. "Do you want me to read the directions for you?"

Mrs. Huff answered. "You don't have to read for him, Amy. It will be good practice for him. And you can be setting the table for lunch."

People were always telling Mitchell he could read, but somehow he had trouble believing them. If he could read, *really* read, not just stumble along in an easy book, why was he always in the slowest reading group in his class?

But Mitchell was not a boy to stay downhearted long. He studied the printing on the pudding-mix box, which was much smaller than the printing in a *Think and Do* book.

"Sound out the hard words if you have trouble," said his mother, who was taking a package of hamburger out of the refrigerator. His mother was always telling him to sound out words.

"Aw, Mom, it isn't that hard to read." Mitchell tore open the package and emptied the pudding mix into the bowl of the mixer and consulted the directions again before he took a bottle of milk from the refrigerator and carefully added two cups of milk to the yellow powder in the bowl. Once more he consulted the directions, reading each word slowly and carefully and feeling pleased that he really could understand the words and do what they told him.

Next he took an egg from a carton in the refrigerator and cracked it gently against the bowl. He pushed his two thumbs against the cracked place, and the whole side of the shell caved in. Mitchell quickly held the egg over the bowl while the white ran out of the shell. "Yipe!" yelped Mitchell, bringing Amy to look over his shoulder.

"Mom!" cried Amy. "Mitchell is putting *egg* in the pudding. He isn't supposed to put egg in instant pudding!"

"You are, too. It says so on the box." The rest of the egg, shell and all, slipped out of his fingers into the bowl. "Now see what you made me do."

"It does *not* say you're supposed to put egg in the pudding," insisted Amy. "I've made instant pudding millions of times, and I know." She snatched up the box while Mitchell wiped his eggy fingers on his jeans.

Mitchell grabbed the box away from his sister. "I'm making this pudding," he informed her.

"All right, let's not have a battle," said Mrs. Huff. "Read it out loud, Mitchell."

" 'Empty two cups of cold milk into bowl. Sprinkle contents of package over milk. Beat with egg—' " Mitchell, who was usually nervous when reading aloud in front of Amy, was triumphant, but his triumph ended with the next letters printed on the box. " 'Beater,' " he said sheepishly. " 'Beat with egg*beater* for two minutes.' I guess I didn't read far enough."

"See!" said Amy gleefully. "I told you there wasn't any egg in it!" Amy could read anything—pudding directions, newspaper stories in small print, even parts of grown-up books like Dr. Spock's.

"Don't feel bad, Mitchell." Mrs. Huff took a spoon from a drawer and dipped out the eggshell. "I don't see why it shouldn't be good with egg in it. Go ahead and mix it and see what happens."

"Raw egg. Ick," was Amy's comment.

But after Mitchell had run the mixer for two minutes and poured the yellow liquid into bowls, the mixture was still runny and refused to turn into pudding. "Now what do I do?" he asked, disgusted with himself.

"Cook it?" suggested Amy, tilting a bowl to see how runny the pudding was.

"We can try." Mrs. Huff scraped all the pudding into a saucepan and handed Mitchell a spoon. "The egg may thicken it. Keep stirring until it begins to bubble, and we'll see what happens."

"Quit breathing in it," said Mitchell, when Amy leaned over the pan to watch. "We don't want any of your cooties in the pudding." Amy backed away, and Mitchell stirred round and round until the mixture began to steam and then to bubble. He lifted a spoonful and watched the pudding trickle back into the pan. "Nope," he said unhappily. "It isn't going to work. I wrecked the pudding."

Mrs. Huff took the spoon and stirred a moment before removing the pan from the heat. "I'm afraid you're right. It isn't going to thicken."

Mitchell glared at Amy. If she started making fun of him, teasing him about stopping at "egg" when he should have gone on and read "egg-beater," poking fun at the runny pudding. . . . All Mitchell could think was *Pow!* and Mitchell was not supposed to hit his sister. Hitting was one thing his parents were very strict about, but it was a temptation sometimes. "Stupid old knuckle-headed me," he muttered. If Amy was such a good reader, she could do the reading. He didn't care.

"Oh, come on, Mitch. It isn't as bad as all that," said Amy. "We could put it into glasses and drink it. Like a milk shake only different."

"Sure," agreed Mitchell, relaxing. "It would still taste like pudding, and that way we wouldn't have to waste it." He never could tell about Amy. Sometimes she did just the opposite of what he expected.

After a lunch of hamburgers topped off by a glass of lukewarm lemon pudding, Mitchell said, "Well, so long, Mom. I think I'll go ride my bike."

"Oh, no, you don't. Not yet," said his mother. "Follow me into the living room."

"But, Mom, don't you want me to get any exercise and fresh air?" Mitchell asked, hoping to divert his mother.

"Not right now," said Mrs. Huff cheerfully. "Not until you read two pages aloud to me."

"Do you want me to grow up weak and puny?" Mitchell asked.

"Certainly," agreed Mrs. Huff. "A weak, puny good reader."

"Oh, Mom, cut it out." Mitchell could not help laughing as he followed his mother into the living room. He decided to try a different tactic. "How about Amy going over her multiplication tables?" he asked.

"Because right now we are talking about you, not Amy," said his mother.

Mitchell flopped down on the couch beside his mother. Everyone seemed to have something to say about his reading. His third-grade teacher had written on his progress report that reading aloud during the summer should help him move up to a higher reading group in the fourth grade.

"All you need is practice to help you gain confidence," his mother kept telling him.

"We're glad to help you, Mitch. That's what we're here for," his father repeated almost every day.

"It isn't hard, Mitch. Really it isn't," Amy insisted.

Well, maybe reading was easy for Amy, but it wasn't for Mitchell. Reading was not only difficult, it was embarrassing because Mitchell suspected everyone of thinking, How come Mitchell is in the low reading group when his twin sister can read any old thing she wants to?

Mitchell glowered at the book that his mother opened and spread between them. Just because he had to read did not mean he was going to like it. " 'Jeff climbed up on the pony,' " he read to his mother while thinking, Stupid old babyish Jeff who rode a pony instead of a horse.

"Climbed up on what kind of pony?" interrupted his mother.

Mitchell stared at the sentence he had just read.

What was wrong this time? It sounded right to him.

"Look at each word as you read," said his mother, as she had said many, many times before.

" 'Climbed up on *his* pony,' " corrected Mitchell with a sigh. The pony, his pony. What difference did it make?

"That's right!" said his mother, as if Mitchell had done something remarkable. Well, she wasn't fooling him even for a minute. He hadn't. Mitchell liked stories, but he liked good stories like those his mother read aloud—the *Jungle Book* and the book about Robin Hood with the old-fashioned words like "odd's bodkin."

At that point Amy came into the room with a book in her hand, a book three times as thick as Mitchell's. She sat down in a chair and began to read.

Mitchell scowled, but continued reading the story of Jeff riding his pony along with the ranch hands who were driving a herd of cattle. He must have skipped a word in a sentence, because suddenly what he was reading did not make sense.

"Guess what page I'm on now!" exclaimed Amy, interrupting.

"Mom!" cried Mitchell. "Does *she* have to be in here when I'm reading?" Amy never hesitated to let people know she was in the fastest reading group in her class.

"I'm on page ninety-two," announced Amy.

"I'll bet that book doesn't begin on page one," said Mitchell. "I'll bet it begins on about page twenty."

"It begins on page eleven."

"Then you haven't read ninety-two pages," said Mitchell hotly.

"Amy, why don't you read in your room for a while?" suggested Mrs. Huff.

"But, Mom, it's more comfortable in here," protested Amy with an innocence that did not fool Mitchell. He knew there was something about his having to read aloud that always brought out the worst in his sister.

For a minute Mitchell was hopeful. If an argument developed he might get out of reading. But no, Mrs. Huff sent Amy off to her room where, Mitchell noticed, she did not close her door. Grimly he read on, disliking Jeff and his pony more with each word. He read, his mother corrected, and a single paragraph seemed to take hours. Mitchell squirmed and picked at the rubber sole of his sneaker.

"Go on, Mitchell," urged his mother. "Don't let Amy bother you. Just remember, some things are easier for girls than for boys."

Maybe his mother was right, but all the important things seemed to be easy for girls. Nobody talked about boys being in the highest ball-throwing group.

Mitchell plodded on until he thought of a way to give himself a rest. He looked up from the book and said rapidly, "Is your family getting the vitamins it needs? Eat Superbread, the bread enriched with one million vitamins to help your children grow!"

"What on earth—" began Mrs. Huff.

"That's the commercial," explained Mitchell.

"Oh, Mitchell—" Mrs. Huff laughed as Amy, book in hand, came back to the living room to see what was funny. "Please. Spare us commercials in books. That's one place we're safe from them."

Mitchell, who had gained a moment of rest from reading, knew he was dangerously close to a lecture on the evils of television. His mother often said that if it weren't for the French Chef they would get rid of the television set. While Amy settled herself once more in the living room Mitchell quickly returned to stupid old babyish Jeff and words, words, words. Words with endings that had to be looked at carefully. Mean words that looked like one thing, but if he missed a single letter somehow turned into something quite different. Little words that didn't seem worth bothering with, but if Mitchell failed to bother with them, suddenly the whole sentence was saying something it was not supposed to say. And the worst part of the whole thing was it was all so boring and babyish. Stupid old babyish Jeff. Nobody ever broke up Jeff's skate board and threw the pieces at him. Nobody ever tried to get Jeff. Oh no. Old Jeff rode around on his pony, and anybody could tell from the pictures that everything turned out just dandy.

"Mom, I've been reading for hours," Mitchell finally protested, when he had sent Amy into giggles by reading "stamper" when the word was "stampede." "Can I stop now?"

Mrs. Huff smiled in a tired sort of way. "It's only been ten minutes. Come on, finish this page."

Mitchell flopped back on the couch, his eyes

closed and his tongue hanging out to show his mother how exhausted he was.

"You poor boy," Mrs. Huff pretended sympathy. "Come on, pull yourself together. There are only four more lines."

Four more horrible lines full of horrible words about stupid old babyish Jeff and his stupid old babyish pony. Mitchell groaned and tried not to think, Stupid old babyish me.

"Guess what page I'm on *now?*" said Amy.

Mitchell was not going to take any more remarks from Amy. He was in no mood to listen to his sister brag about being on page ten million. "You keep quiet!" he yelled, sitting up.

"I don't have to!" Amy yelled back.

"Now Amy, stop interrupting," said Mrs. Huff. "Mitchell is reading."

Encouraged because his mother was on his side, Mitchell decided to tear into those four lines and get them over. He held the book, so that his mother could not see the text and slow him down with corrections, and read as rapidly as he could, " 'The cattle were frightened. They began to run. Jeff saw someone coming. "Look!" said Jeff. "Here come our fiends." ' " There. Mitchell had finished the page, and fiends was one mistake he had made on purpose.

"Fiends?" said Mrs. Huff, while the sound of Amy's laughter floated across her book. "Mitchell, look again."

His mother and Amy did not understand that he had deliberately made a mistake, because any boy would rather read a book about fiends than a book about friends, but did the people who wrote books know this fact? No, they did not. They were too dumb just as his mother and sister were too dumb to know when he made a mistake on purpose. Mitchell held the book up close to his face and glared at the word. " ' "Here come our *friends*." ' " He finished with a yell and slammed the book.

"That's right, Mitchell," said his mother calmly. "All you have to do is look at the words carefully."

"Stamper," Amy said softly to herself and giggled.

"You shut up!" yelled Mitchell.

"Now children," said Mrs. Huff. "You know, Mitchell, it's too bad stamper isn't a real word—a sort of combination of scamper and stampede.

And now why don't you go outside and play?"

Amy put down her book. "Yes, Mitch," she said, "why don't you stamper out and play?"

"That's enough, Amy." Mrs. Huff spoke sharply.

Mitchell managed to give Amy a quick sidewise kick as he walked past her on his way to his room. He could not possibly have hurt her because he was wearing sneakers, but still Amy said, "Mom, Mitchell kicked me!" as she stuck one foot out in front of her brother.

Mitchell was too quick for her. "Tattletale," he said, sidestepping. "And stop trying to trip me." This did not count as tattling, because he was speaking to his sister and not to his mother.

"Mitchell, don't kick your sister. Amy, stop teasing your brother." Mrs. Huff picked up a library book of her own and began to read.

"Funny little boy," said Amy in her annoying pat-the-little-fellow-on-the-head voice.

"Hah!" said Mitchell darkly. "You can't call me little. I'm taller than you."

"But I'm older," said Amy, sitting up straight.

"Ten minutes is all," scoffed Mitchell.

"Ten minutes, but I'm still the oldest." Amy

was not ready to let the argument die. "You'll never be as old as I am. Never, never, never!"

"Shut up!" yelled Mitchell, because he had no answer.

Mrs. Huff looked up from her book. "Children, stop this instant."

"He started it!" "She started it!" Mitchell and Amy spoke at the same time. They tried again. "Well, he did!" "Well, she did!" Still they spoke in unison. They glared at one another, each silently daring the other to speak first.

"Icka bicka backa soda cracker," said Mrs. Huff, and went on with her reading.

Mitchell and Amy looked at one another in surprise.

"Mom, what are you talking about?" asked Amy. "What do soda crackers have to do with it?"

"Don't you know?" asked Mrs. Huff. "It's a counting rhyme we used when I was about your age. I think of it every time you two start fighting."

"How does it go?" Amy was always interested in rhymes. Maybe that was why she was such a good reader. Beginning back in the first grade, reading workbooks were great on rhymes. Cat, take away *c* and put an *r* in its place and what do you have? Rat. Amy had always enjoyed that sort of thing.

Mrs. Huff began to recite,

> "My mother, your mother,
> Live across the way.
> Fifteen-sixteen East Broadway.
> Every night they have a fight
> And this is what they say.
> Icka bicka backa soda cracker
> Out goes she."

Amy was delighted and picked up the verse at once. "My mother, your mother, live across the way—"

The fight was over, the out-loud part of it, but Mitchell went right on fighting in his thoughts. Icka bicka backa soda cracker, out goes Amy, he thought crossly, as he went into the kitchen and grabbed a banana and stuffed it into his pocket before he left the house and wheeled his bicycle out of the garage.

When Mitchell reached the street, he pedaled as hard as he could; pumping his legs up and down made him feel better. First Alan and the skate board. Then the runny pudding. And then Amy hearing him make a stupid mistake like stamper. She thought she was so good, reading all those thick books while he stumbled around in thin books. Well, Amy was good, and Mitchell had to admit that he was proud of her. The trouble was, he wanted to be proud of himself, too.

Pumping a bicycle in a hilly neighborhood was hard work, and Mitchell gradually slowed down. Oh well, he thought, as he pulled the banana out of his pocket, things were sure to be better in the fourth grade. When he came to a level spot in the street he rode without using the handlebars while he peeled the banana and stuffed the skin into his pocket. He must remember to throw the skin into the garbage can, he thought as he pedaled along. Last week his mother had put a pair of jeans through the washing machine with a banana skin in the pocket.

4

AMY AND THE AUDIO-VISUAL AIDS

AFTERWARDS Amy was sorry for the way she had behaved when Mitchell was struggling to read aloud. She really did not want to hurt his feelings, but whenever she saw him sitting there on the couch with their mother she could not help feeling left out. Acting that way was silly, she knew, because reading aloud was a chore for Mitchell, just as multiplication tables were a chore for her, a chore she managed to avoid until the day finally arrived that she and Mitchell had waited for so long, their first day in the fourth grade.

As Amy had hoped, the morning turned out to

be foggy, with moisture dripping like rain from the eucalyptus trees. By noon the sun would be out, but in the meantime Amy had a good excuse to wear her new pleated skirt, which was just enough too long to make her feel like a ten-year-old instead of a nine-year-old. Amy noticed that Mitchell, who had been saying that school was a bad word, was in a hurry to leave that first morning, and she wondered if he was trying to avoid Alan Hibbler. Mitchell had not mentioned the skate-board incident again, but Amy had not forgotten it and she was sure her brother had not forgotten it either.

"By, Mom!" Mitchell yelled, and ran out the back door in his new jeans, size nine slim.

Amy left for school shortly after Mitchell had disappeared into the fog. She was too happy and excited to wait any longer, but instead of running as if she had springs in the soles of her sneakers, she walked sedately, enjoying the feel of her new skirt brushing against the back of her knees and secretly hoping that people would think, There goes a girl who is one decade old. Marla joined her, and she too walked sedately in her new pleated skirt. They acted very grown-up to the traffic boy, who led them across the street nearest to the school.

Familiar old Bay View School sat solidly in the midst of uproar and confusion. During the summer, construction of a new wing had started and concrete mixers rattled and growled at one end of the building. Temporary wooden classrooms covered half the playground, which swarmed with screaming, yelling boys and girls, most of them wearing new school clothes and all of them excited at seeing old friends. Amy glanced quickly around and located Mitchell playing kickball at one end of the playground and Alan Hibbler running through a second-grade girls' hopscotch game at the other.

Still trying to behave like ten-year-olds, Amy and Marla climbed the steps of the temporary wooden building that was to be Mrs. Martin's classroom until the new wing was completed. "It's like going to an old-fashioned school," remarked Amy, who had attended the third grade in the main building.

"I know," agreed Marla. "I feel sort of like Laura in the *Little House* books."

"We've walked miles across the prairie," said Amy.

Marla took up the game. "With our scarves over the lower part of our faces to keep our noses from freezing."

Amy objected. "Not on the first day of school, silly. Nobody's nose ever froze on the first day of school."

"I guess you're right," said Marla. "Leave out the scarves. Make it with our lunches in baskets instead. And sunbonnets on our heads."

Amy soon discovered there was nothing old-fashioned about the inside of the temporary classroom. Boys and girls were crowding around a lot of new equipment—a television set, a tape recorder, a record player, a slide projector and a screen.

"Hey! TV at school!" said Mike Melnick, who had followed the girls up the steps.

"Hi, Amy! Did you know we were going to have TV in school?" asked Bonnie Puckett, who was Amy's next-to-best friend.

"Mrs. Martin will never let us watch anything good," Marla reminded them. "Just educational programs and stuff like that."

"These are our audio-visual aids," Mrs. Martin explained, after her new class had saluted the flag. "*Audio* means to hear and *visual* means to see. Our audio-visual aids will help us to learn with our ears and our eyes." To demonstrate one of the ways in which the new equipment could be used, she put a record on the phonograph, and the class heard someone playing *America the Beautiful* on the piano to accompany their morning song.

Amy enjoyed singing to the record, and from the temporary building next door she could hear Mitchell's room singing to their recording of *America the Beautiful*. She decided that audio-visual aids might be fun in spite of being educational. She knew that Mitchell would think so, because he liked anything that could be plugged in and turned on.

Amy was even more pleased with the audio-visual aids as the day went on. When class elections were held and all the hands were counted, Amy was elected vice-president. She looked modestly at her hands in her lap while Mrs. Martin explained that it was the duty of the vice-president to play the record of *America the Beautiful* each morning after the president led the flag salute. Amy was proud of her new responsibility. In the third grade the class vice-president just sat around waiting for the president to get sick.

"Lucky!" whispered Marla from across the aisle.

Amy's pleasure lasted until arithmetic, which was a review of multiplication facts. Mrs. Martin hinted at a test in the near future.

"Ee-yew, a test," said Amy, as she and Marla lined up to go to the cafetorium for lunch.

"Multiplication, icky," agreed Marla. "Ee-yew" and "icky" were popular expressions of dislike with fourth-grade girls.

That evening at dinner Amy started to tell about all the new audio-visual aids when Mitchell interrupted. "Guess what?" he said. "Miss Colby didn't tell us what to do in arithmetic. She turned on the tape recorder, and her voice told us what to do."

"Mitchell," said Amy sternly. "*I* was talking."

"Well, she did," said Mitchell. "And when the cement trucks and the workmen made too much noise we got to recite into a microphone. Or we did until the class in the building next door plugged in their slide projector and blew a fuse. After that we just shouted above the noise."

"Mom. Dad—" protested Amy, eager to tell about her audio-visual aids before Mitchell told everything.

"Ladies and gentlemen," said Mitchell, speaking into a fork as if it were a microphone. "This is your friendly neighborhood fourth grader. Six times six is thirty-six. Six times seven is forty-two."

That Mitchell, thought Amy, amused in spite of herself at her brother's performance. He could be so exasperating, bringing multiplication into the conversation purposely to annoy her.

"Mitchell," said Mr. Huff. "Amy was speaking."

With a triumphant look at Mitchell, Amy told about her duty as vice-president. "And we're going to get to watch TV, too," she said. When she saw that her parents did not share her enthusiasm, she added hastily, "Of course, it will be educational."

"Our teacher is going to give us a test on multiplication facts to help decide which arithmetic group we belong in," announced Mitchell.

Amy braced herself, knowing Mitchell must feel

this way when she told what page she was on while he was reading aloud.

"What about your class, Amy?" asked her father. "Aren't you going to have an arithmetic test, too?"

"Ee-yew," answered Amy, wrinkling her nose.

"That hardly answers the question."

"Well, yes," admitted Amy.

"Seven times four," her father shot at her. He was an accountant who was probably born knowing his multiplication tables.

"Twenty-eight," Mitchell answered promptly.

"Twenty-eight," echoed Amy, relieved that her brother had supplied the answer for her.

"Mitchell, let Amy answer. Five times nine."

"Um. Um—" Amy was trying to think.

"Everybody knows fives," said Mitchell.

"Five times nine is—um—forty-six. No, forty-*five*." Amy hoped her father would forget about multiplication now.

"Amy, I think that we had better go over your tables this evening. You practice your cello while I do the dishes, and then I'll help you," said Mrs. Huff. "And Mitchell, you had better read aloud for a little while."

Mitchell groaned. "Do I gotta?"

"Yes, you gotta," answered his mother, and Mitchell groaned again.

Amy sat through the rest of the meal positively hating the multiplication tables. She was not like Mitchell, who might squirm and dawdle and think up interruptions, but would eventually do the things he did not want to do. When Amy did not want to do something, she did not want to do it one hundred percent. She simply did not want to learn her multiplication tables. They were so *boring*, as boring as visiting the post office with her old Brownie troop or having to sit quietly while grown-ups talked politics. Oh, she understood *about* multiplication all right. She had made graphs and done all the things that were supposed to make third graders understand the *reasons* for multiplication, but when she came to sitting down and memorizing them, Amy balked. Ask Amy three times four, and she would rather write down imaginary fours three times and add them up in her head than memorize a lot of boring old tables. Mitchell's popping out with the right answer ahead of her didn't help either. "Twelve!" Mitchell would say while Amy was still writing imagi-

nary fours on an imaginary blackboard with imaginary chalk.

By skillful management Amy managed to avoid
reviewing the multiplication tables that evening.
She set the timer on the kitchen clock to mark the
half hour that she and Mitchell must practice their
music. Then she played her cello with unusual dili-
gence. When Mitchell struggled to blow the right
notes of *The Red River Valley* on his French
horn, she did not yield to the temptation to play
the tune correctly on her cello. Nothing made
Mitchell madder than having Amy play correctly
by ear the music he was trying to play by note.
As he so often reminded her, the French horn was
the most difficult of the brass instruments.

When the timer ping-ping-pinged at the end of
the half hour, Amy let Mitchell beat her into the
kitchen to turn it off and instead skipped into the
bathroom to take a bath without being told.

Amy spent a long time in the bathtub while
out in the living room she could hear Mitchell
plodding along with the story about Jeff and his
pony. She lay back and was glad she was not out
there trying to add up an imaginary column of six
eights while her mother said, "*Think*, Amy." Her

mother always confused her by saying, "*Think*, Amy," when she was halfway up the imaginary column, and then she had to start over again.

"Amy, what are you doing in there?" Mrs. Huff called through the bathroom door.

"Taking a bath," answered Amy virtuously.

"Well, hurry up about it," said her mother.

After her bath Amy brushed her teeth with careful up-and-down strokes while she ran the water so hard she could not hear her mother tell her to hurry. After that she had to fasten a dental rubber band to the retainer she was wearing to straighten her teeth. With one thing and another the evening slipped by. Then it was bedtime, and there was no time for multiplication tables.

"You know, Amy," said Mrs. Huff, when she had kissed her daughter good-night, "you're never going to learn your multiplication tables until you really want to learn them. There is nothing I can do to help until you decide to learn them."

"Mm-hm," murmured Amy sleepily. Nothing would ever make her want to learn her multiplication tables. Nothing.

Somehow, there was no time for multiplication in the morning either. In the midst of breakfast

Mitchell remembered he was supposed to take some money to school for insurance in case he was injured during school hours while he was in the fourth grade. Amy said she was supposed to take insurance money, too, and there was confusion while Mrs. Huff wrote checks and Amy and her brother found the forms to be filled out. When school insurance was taken care of, Amy suddenly remembered she needed an old peanut-butter jar to use in a science experiment—the class was going to sprout beans in such a way that their growth could be watched through the jars. Then Mitchell reminded his mother that they both needed money to pay for their lunches, which meant a search for the exact change to pay for two lunches so they would not slow up the line in the cafetorium.

"Good-by. Have a nice day." Mrs. Huff sounded a little tired as Amy followed her brother out the back door with her lunch money, check for accident insurance, and the peanut-butter jar. "And after this, please remember things the night before," she called after them.

"Sure, Mom," Mitchell called back, light-footed in his new sneakers.

"Sure, Mom," answered Amy, lighthearted because once again she had escaped drill in her multi-plication facts. The fall morning was the kind she liked best—patches of sun shining through the morning fog and the pungent smell of damp euca-lyptus leaves heavy in the air. Who could care about multiplication on a morning like this one?

School started happily enough with Amy setting the phonograph needle in the right groove of the *America the Beautiful* record, but when the class had sung the song and Amy had returned to her seat, Mrs. Martin started passing out paper. "Class, we are going to have our test on multiplication facts the first thing while our minds are fresh."

There was a murmur in the classroom. A lot of pupils felt Mrs. Martin was not being fair. Amy had a sinking feeling in her stomach that felt like the sound her cello made when she dragged her bow across the strings.

"Mrs. Martin, there aren't any problems on my paper. Just rows of numbers," someone said.

Mrs. Martin smiled. "I have a surprise for you. Today a phonograph record is going to give us our problems. The numbers on your papers are the numbers of the problems. You all know enough to put your first answer by number one."

This procedure was a surprise to Amy, who had not expected an audio-visual aid to give tests.

Fog still hung like a gray veil outside the windows of the little wooden building. Mrs. Martin turned on the lights. "When we all have our papers in front of us and our pencils in our hands, I will play a record of a man reading the multiplication problems. Can anyone tell me why we are taking our test this way?"

"So we get to use our audio-visual aids?" suggested Mike, who was always the first one in the class to speak.

"So you can do something else while we take the tests?" asked Bonnie Puckett.

Mrs. Martin shook her head. "We're taking the test from the record, because all the fourth-grade classes are going to take the same test and it is important for all classes to be tested at the same speed. This way one teacher cannot read the problems faster than another teacher."

Amy had to admit to herself that this reason sounded fair, but still she did not like the idea. She held her pencil beside the first space on her paper so she would be ready.

Mrs. Martin set the record on the turntable.

"Let me give you a hint," she said. "If you don't know an answer, skip it and go on to the next problem." Then she set the needle in the groove on the record.

"Are you ready?" asked the phonograph in a man's voice. His voice was as calm as the voice on the birdcall record. Here was another man who had never hit his sister or cheered at a baseball game.

"No!" shouted the class.

The record ignored this response. "Four times six," it said, sounding so much like the man on Mrs. Huff's birdcall record that for a moment Amy expected to hear a chirp or a trill. Four times six, four times six, Amy thought frantically. I can do it if you'll just give me time.

The record did not care how Amy felt. It was not interested in giving her time. "Three times five," it said evenly.

Wait! a voice within Amy cried. I don't have four times six yet. She could hear Mike Melnick's pencil scratch on his paper. Mike knew four times six. Mike also knew three times five. Mike was the smartest boy in the class.

"Five times eight." The record was not inter-

ested in what Mike or Amy or anyone else knew.
It had no heart. It isn't fair, thought Amy rebel-
liously. The record doesn't ask anything I can
answer fast.

"Two times two," said the record.

Four! thought Amy triumphantly in spite of
her dismay that the record seemed to read her
thoughts. She managed to write down the answer
and think, I got you that time.

The record, ignoring her turmoil, said, "Six
times six." Before she even had time to think it
went on and said, "Four times five."

This answer Amy knew, but when she wrote it
down she was not sure she wrote it in the right
space.

"Three times nine," said the machine.

I *hate* you, thought Amy, growing more and
more panicky. If a real live teacher had been giving
the test, she could have raised her hand and asked
to have the problem repeated in order to gain time.
All around her she heard pencils scratch on paper.
Knowing that Marla was able to write down answers hurt, and Amy felt as if Marla were almost
disloyal to get ahead of her. "Nine times two." If
only you would stop for a minute so I could catch

up, thought Amy. Just one teeny little weeny little minute. That's all I ask.

"Seven times four," said the relentless machine, feeling not the least bit sorry for Amy.

Seven times four, seven times four. Amy's thoughts were spinning. I hate you, I hate you, I *hate* you. She had forgotten all the multiplication facts she had ever known. All she could do was sit and hate the machine for not caring and herself for not knowing the answers.

Amy gave up. Her eyes filled with tears. Everyone in the class would finish the test but Amy. She would be put in the lowest arithmetic group, and all because of that machine. It wasn't fair. She never thought an audio-visual aid could treat her this way. The fourth grade had started out so happily, too, in the little building like an old-fashioned school. Well, no pioneer girl in a book ever had to take a test from a machine that would not slow down.

"Three times four."

Oh shut up, thought Amy, blinking away her tears. Her pride was hurt. Now Marla was better than she was in arithmetic. And Mitchell was sure to shine in a test given by a machine, the way he loved things that plugged in and turned on. Amy was left behind.

Suddenly the lights went out. "Fi-ive—" drawled the machine. Amy looked up from her paper. "—t-ime-ss—se-ev-en-n-n," the machine dragged the words out, before it died. Amy flopped back in her seat, glad of a moment's rest.

"Hooray!" said Mike Melnick right out loud, and the rest of the class laughed.

"Oh dear. And right in the middle of our test," said Mrs. Martin.

Of course, everyone was delighted, and when Mrs. Martin sent Mike into Miss Colby's room to find out if her lights had gone out too, they learned that in all the temporary buildings the electricity had gone off because Miss Colby had blown a fuse when she had plugged in her slide projector. She had already notified the custodian. Minutes went by and still the lights did not go on. Finally a message arrived saying the custodian was out of fuses and had to drive downtown for a new supply.

"I'm sorry this had to happen," said Mrs. Martin. "There is nothing we can do but start the test another time. Pass in your papers, please."

Amy went limp with relief. She hoped the

school would be without electricity for a long, long time, perhaps forever. After all, why did they need it? Pioneers managed without electricity, didn't they? The thought crossed her mind that she had never read any stories about pioneer girls balking at their multiplication tables either. Pioneer girls were always thirsty for learning.

That afternoon when Amy returned home she found her mother listening to the birdcall record. "Bobwhite," said the man's calm voice from the spinning record. "*Bobwhite. Bobwhite. Ka-loi-kee,*" answered the bird. Amy dropped into a chair. For a moment she had expected the bird to say, "Six times seven."

"Why, what's the matter, Amy?" Mrs. Huff sounded concerned as she turned off the phonograph.

"Nothing," said Amy sadly. She enjoyed being alone with her mother, but the memory of the test on multiplication facts spoiled everything.

"Yes, there is. Something is bothering you. I can tell."

Amy managed a half smile. "I just . . . expected the bird to say something else, is all."

Mitchell's sneakers came pounding up the driveway, and Amy heard her brother burst in through the kitchen door.

"Hi, lucky people," said Mitchell, appearing in the living room, banana in hand and his shirttail hanging out.

Amy knew at once from the cheerful look on her brother's face and from the jaunty way in which he peeled his banana that everything was all right. Alan Hibbler had not bullied Mitchell that day.

"Hello, Mitchell. What kind of day did you have?" asked his mother.

"Pretty good," said Mitchell through a mouthful of banana.

"I'm glad to hear that," said his mother. "Don't take such big bites."

"We had a keen test in arithmetic this afternoon," said Mitchell, when he had gulped down the bite of banana. "It was on a record and—"

"Oh, be quiet," Amy muttered under her breath, more annoyed with herself than with her brother. Mitchell should talk. He knew his multiplication facts. He *liked* multiplication facts.

Unfortunately, Mitchell caught her remark and

became dramatic. When Mitchell was feeling good about something, he was inclined to be dramatic. "How do you like that?" he demanded. "Here I am, minding my own business, eating a banana, when my stupid old sister—"

"I am not your stupid old sister! And you shut up!" Amy flared up, arguing out of habit. She had not been angry with Mitchell and was quite certain that he was not angry with her. Still, she couldn't very well let him call her his stupid old sister and get away with it.

"I don't have to shut up," Mitchell informed his sister. "This is a free country, isn't it?"

"It doesn't mean it's a free country to call people names," said Amy, taking up the familiar argument.

Mitchell was all exaggerated innocence. "What did I do? I just walk in here, minding my own business, eating a banana, and all of a sudden my stupid old sister tells me to be quiet."

Mrs. Huff groaned. "Both of you, be quiet! Mitchell, stop teasing. Amy, you were rude. And as for me, I'm tired of your old 'it's-a-free-country' argument. It has been going on since kindergarten."

Mitchell was irrepressible. "Okay, Mom. I guess Amy hasn't heard of freedom of speech."

Now Amy turned dramatic. "Mom! You see what I mean? Freedom of speech doesn't mean freedom to—"

Mrs. Huff interrupted. "Let me tell you something. Mothers are free to tell their children to stop bickering. Now both of you go to your rooms until you calm down."

In her room Amy sat down and faced the unpleasant truth. Mitchell had no trouble with the test because he knew the answers, and she could not let her brother get ahead of her. She was going to have to learn her multiplication facts and she was going to have to learn them fast, because sooner or later she would have to face that record player again, and the only way to beat it was to know the answers. Amy got up and rummaged through a drawer full of jacks, yo-yos, a plastic box of baby teeth, her junior fire marshal's badge, and a lot of old birthday cards until she found the bundle of multiplication flash cards she had made in the third grade. They were not really cards but slips of paper with a multiplication problem on one side and the answer on the other.

For the first time, as she slipped the rubber band from the packet, Amy really wanted to learn the multiplication tables. If Mitchell and Marla and everyone else could keep up with a machine, she could too. She would overcome this hardship by being a brave pioneer girl huddled in front of the fireplace while the blizzard raged and the wolves howled . . . she was thirsty for learning. . . .

A sound caught Amy's attention, and she looked up just in time to see Mitchell's arm reach around from his room, which was next to hers. A paper airplane came sailing onto her bed. The airplane bore one word printed in large letters with a ball-point pen. The word was *Stoopid*.

Amy giggled and was about to say in her pat-the-little-fellow-on-the-head voice, "Funny little boy. Doesn't even know how to spell stupid," but instead she settled down to face a cold winter evening of hardship testing herself on multiplication facts while the howling wolves moved closer and closer to the little log cabin in the clearing in the forest. . . .

Mitchell's eyes appeared around the door jamb to see how his sister was reacting to the message on the airplane.

"Hi," said Amy calmly. "I'm working on my multiplication facts."

"No kidding?" The rest of Mitchell appeared in the doorway. "Want me to hold the flash cards?" he asked.

"Sure." Amy handed her brother the bundle of slips. Mitchell would never confuse her by saying, "*Think*, Amy," the way her mother did. They would both huddle in front of the fireplace while the wolves moved closer and closer. . . .

5

A BAD TIME FOR MITCHELL

WHILE Amy was enduring the hardships of learning her multiplication tables, Mitchell was having troubles of his own in the fourth grade. Every morning after breakfast Mitchell brushed his teeth and practiced his French horn until he felt dizzy, as if he had been blowing up balloons. Then he made his bed, pounding down the lumps with his fist, and threw his pajamas either under the bed or into the closet. "By, Mom!" he yelled and ran out the back door, eager to avoid Alan Hibbler and get to school in time to play kickball before the bell rang. Now that temporary buildings took up so much of the play space, he had to get to school early if he hoped to get into a game.

After the bell rang Mitchell's troubles began. His reading workbook fairly blushed with red marks made by Miss Colby's pencil. The girls in his reading group giggled when he read "mountain tail" instead of "mountain trail."

When his class wrote compositions pretending they were rats on Sir Francis Drake's ship at the time California was discovered, Mitchell's paper was returned with the spelling of almost every word corrected. He did not think Miss Colby was fair to expect correct spelling and an interesting story at the same time, especially when the story was supposed to have been written by a rat.

Mitchell dreaded the weekly trip to the school library, where everyone was required to take out a book. While the rest of his class browsed, Mitchell passed the time spinning the globe of the world and thinking how interesting life would be if the earth turned so fast that people who forgot to hang on would go spinning off into space—Alan Hibbler, for instance.

When the period was almost over, Miss Colby always asked, "Mitchell, have you found a book yet?" and Mitchell would grab a thick book on chemistry or electricity because nobody was going to catch Mitchell Huff carrying around any babyish book.

And then there was Bernadette Stumpf, the new girl who was given Bill Collins's desk across the aisle. Miss Colby moved Bill to the other side of the room, because she said he and Mitchell paid too much attention to one another and not enough to their workbooks. Bernadette was a small wiry girl with a lot of long witchy black hair, and on the first day of school she wore only one sock. Mitchell could not help staring at Bernadette's feet. Finally when he could stand his curiosity no longer, he asked, "How come you're wearing only one sock?"

"I couldn't find the other," answered Bernadette.

"I know what you mean," answered Mitchell, who often had trouble finding socks himself, usually because he had thrown his dirty socks under his bed instead of into the hamper. After that he looked at Bernadette's feet the first thing every morning to see if she had found both her socks. Sometimes she had, but often she wore one girl's sock and one boy's sock or two boy's socks, because, as she said, she had a lot of brothers and there were always boy's socks around the house.

Mitchell thought that a girl who was so careless about socks would be in his reading group, but no, Bernadette tackled everything she had to do with a sort of furious energy that put her in the fast reading group and the first arithmetic group. She was also good at kickball and streaked around the bases with her black hair flying, which was fortunate because none of the girls wanted to jump rope with her. Mitchell finally formed a grudging admiration for Bernadette, a girl who obviously did not care what others thought of her socks. Amy and her friends were always fussing about their clothes, and Amy often telephoned Marla before school, if Marla did not telephone first, to find out what she was going to wear.

One hot windy morning when Mitchell was bounding along in his sneakers down the hill past a grove of eucalyptus trees, he felt something, some small hard object, hit him between his shoulder blades. He paid no attention because in the heat and the wind, eucalyptus buds were dropping all around him. When he was struck between the shoulder blades a second time, he stopped and turned. Alan Hibbler was bounding along behind him in *his* sneakers. Farther on up the hill Amy and Marla were coming around a bend in the street.

"Hi, there, kid," said Alan, stopping to scoop up a handful of eucalyptus buds.

"Hi," said Mitchell, and went on springing down the hill. Just as he expected, a eucalyptus bud sailed past his shoulder and then another and another. Mitchell's father, when he had heard the story of the skate board, said there were two things to do about a bully, ignore him or fight him. Mitchell could not see any sense in fighting so he ignored the buds. He did not speed up, he did not slow down, he just continued as if nothing had happened. The next bud hit him in the middle of the back. He ignored it—at least that is the way he hoped he looked to Alan. A eucalyptus bud, which was as big as a marble, was a hard thing to ignore.

More buds came pelting after Mitchell, some hitting him, some flying past him. One struck him right on the back of the neck and that really stung, but Mitchell kept on going. As much as he longed to stop and peg just one bud back at Alan good and hard, he would not let himself. If he ignored Alan long enough, Alan might get tired of bullying and if he did not, well. . . . Mitchell would have to think about that problem when the time came.

Mitchell was pretty angry by the time he reached the intersection nearest the school, where he had to wait for the traffic boy to lead him across the street or get reported. Alan caught up and stood directly behind him.

"Chased you, didn't I?" gloated Alan.

Mitchell gritted his teeth and said nothing. He thought about the spinning globe in the library and imagined what would happen if the world was turning so fast everyone had to make his way to school hand over hand, hanging onto bushes. Then when old Alan tried to throw a eucalyptus bud, he would forget to hold on and go whizzing off into space.

On the way across the street Alan managed to step on Mitchell's heels several times. Grimly Mitchell ignored him. By the time Mitchell got into a kickball game he was so angry and kicked the ball so hard that he made a home run before the fielder had a chance to catch up with the ball. That home run made Mitchell feel a lot better.

Mitchell began to wish he did not have to walk to school, but unfortunately during the summer the mothers of the neighborhood had banded together at a coffee party and vowed that they would no longer drive their children to school unless they had broken legs or heavy musical instruments to carry.

Except for one day a week, when his mother drove the cello and French horn to school, Mitchell walked. He tried different routes to school. Sometimes he succeeded in avoiding Alan, but more often he did not. Eucalyptus buds came flying even when there were no eucalyptus trees nearby, and Mitchell concluded that Alan must keep his pockets stuffed with ammunition. Ignoring Alan became more and more difficult. Sometimes Mitchell felt worn out with ignoring Alan when Alan should have been so tired of being ignored that he would stop bullying.

One evening at dinner Mrs. Huff served a new dish that she had learned to cook by watching the French Chef on television. She said it was stuffed eggplant.

"It looks like a boxing glove cut in half and filled with chopped-up stuff," remarked Mitchell. Speaking of a boxing glove reminded him of Alan Hibbler. "Say, Dad, how about letting me take judo lessons?" he asked.

"I think you're a little young for that," answered his father.

"So you could flip your sister through the air every time you got into an argument?" said Mrs. Huff. "I should say not. Anyway, I do enough chauffeuring as it is. Music lessons, trips to the orthodontist, trips to the shoe store—"

"Oh, never mind," said Mitchell. "It was just one of those out-of-the-question questions."

One hot Friday morning in October, when a dry wind had been rattling the leaves of the eucalyptus trees for days and the temporary classrooms had seemed like ovens in the afternoon, Mitchell consulted the mimeographed school-lunch menu that Mrs. Huff had taped to the inside of a cupboard door. The menu was one thing he had no trouble reading. When he saw what he was to have for lunch, he groaned and said, "Deep Sea Dandies for lunch."

Mrs. Huff laughed. "What on earth are Deep Sea Dandies?"

"An old fish stick in a bun," answered Mitchell. "The cafetorium just tries to make it sound good."

"You mean the ickatorium," corrected Amy.

"So long, Mom," said Mitchell, as he walked out the back door, reluctant to face a day of reading, Deep Sea Dandies, and Alan Hibbler. His sneakers seemed to have lost their bounce, and he plodded down the hill with the muscles between his shoulders tight and tense, waiting for the eucalyptus buds that he was sure would strike. He did not relax once all the way to school, and then, when the traffic boy led him across the street and nothing had happened, he felt let down. Alan had not followed him at all. The thought occurred to Mitchell that Alan was now annoying him as much when he did not follow him as when he did.

"Drat!" said Mitchell, kicking the fence and wishing he knew what to do. The burden of worrying about Alan was wearing him out. In the days that followed he found himself thinking about Alan when he should have been thinking about the history of California or arithmetic. He drew an anchor on the back of his hand with a ball-point pen so he would look tough and tattooed. Miss Colby had to speak to him about wasting time.

One afternoon after school Mitchell walked in the back door, threw his homework and a thick book on electricity down on the kitchen table, and grabbed two bananas out of the wooden bowl on the counter before he went into the living room where his mother was reading her French cookbook.

"Hello, Mitch." Mrs. Huff looked up from her cookbook. Mitchell knew they would probably have something good for dinner that required so much beating, chopping, and straining that his mother would only have time for hamburger patties or canned fruit to go with it. "What kind of day did you have?" his mother asked.

Mitchell flopped into a chair and pulled back the skin on one of his bananas. "Just a day, I guess." He took a big bite of banana and chewed thoughtfully. One thing about bananas, they were easy to chew when he was wearing a dental retainer. They weren't tough, and they didn't have any seeds, pits, or cores to get in the way.

"You don't seem to be your usual happy self

lately," said his mother. "Has something gone wrong?"

For a moment Mitchell was tempted to tell his mother all about Alan, but then he thought better of the impulse. "No, I guess not," said Mitchell. "What could go wrong?"

"Lots of things," said his mother lightly. "Sea-weedy spinach for lunch in the ickatorium, for example."

Mitchell smiled, amused to hear his mother talking like a fourth grader. He broke back the stem of the second banana and pulled down a strip of skin. A banana came in a very neat package.

"Sometimes I think you run on bananas the way a car runs on gasoline," said Mrs. Huff. "Are you sure you aren't worried about something?"

Mitchell made up his mind he was not going to tell his mother about Alan and the eucalyptus buds, because she might call Alan's mother or the principal and get him into more trouble. "Nope," he said after the last bite of banana. "Well, I guess I'll go ride my bike."

Mitchell remembered to put the banana skins in the garbage before he let the back door slam and wheeled his bicycle out of the garage. At the

foot of the steep driveway he headed uphill, pumping as hard as he could. Standing on his pedals and
using every bit of his strength to push them around
made him feel good, and when he made the top of
the hill, he coasted down, enjoying the wind on
his face, until the road rose again and he had to
stand up to pump once more. Panting, he gulped
in lungfuls of air and drove out the stuffy, indoor
feeling that he always had at the end of a school
day or after doing his homework. He even began
to feel better about Alan, who was nothing but
a stupid old bully. Maybe one of these days he
and Alan would have a showdown, good guy
against the bad guy, and the good guy would win
because good guys always won—he hoped. "Pow-
pow-pow," said Mitchell to himself. What were a
few eucalyptus buds anyway? A eucalyptus bud
never hurt anyone. "Pow-pow-pow!"

Feeling more cheerful than he had for some
time, Mitchell rode to the corner where the newspaper carriers gathered to fold their papers across
the street from the real-estate office, but no one
was there yet. He waited a few minutes, watching
some old newspapers blow against the fence, before he rode on, ringing the bell of his bicycle

from time to time just for the satisfaction of making a noise. He cut through the parking lot of a church and headed toward home on a pleasant level street lined with hedges and pine trees. There was no traffic and the street was in bad repair so Mitchell amused himself by weaving in and out among the gravelly patches that showed through the broken asphalt. He was pretending his bicycle was a destroyer working its way around icebergs when he became aware of someone approaching on a bicycle.

It was Alan Hibbler. Oh-oh, thought Mitchell. Here we go again. If there had been a cross street, he would have turned off, but the block was long and there was no way to avoid meeting Alan face-to-face. Since Mitchell could not ignore him this time, he pedaled along, trying to look unconcerned. Maybe, if he was lucky, Alan would be in a hurry. Maybe he was on his way to substitute for one of the paper boys.

"Hi," said Alan, as he stopped his bicycle about twenty feet in front of Mitchell.

"Hi," answered Mitchell, braking his bicycle and putting one foot on the ground. Now what? A showdown like the end of a Western movie?

Mitchell squinted at Alan even though he was not staring into the sun.

"Whatcha doing?" Alan seemed friendly enough.

"Riding around." Mitchell was wary, wondering if Alan had stopped bullying after all. Maybe bullying was something he had outgrown like playing with Tinker Toys or kicking lunch boxes on the school grounds. Or maybe he did not feel so much like a bully when he was alone and face-to-face with Mitchell. Mitchell hooked one thumb in the top of his jeans and waited to see what happened. It just might be that ignoring Alan had worked after all.

"Play you a game of chicken," said Alan.

"How do you play chicken?" asked Mitchell.

Alan explained. "We ride our bikes straight at one another as hard as we can, and the first one to turn aside is chicken."

"What's the point?" asked Mitchell.

"To find out who gets scared and chickens out." Alan was beginning to sound as if he thought Mitchell was not very bright.

"But that's a stupid game," said Mitchell logically. "If nobody turns aside, you've got a couple of wrecked-up bikes and maybe a few broken legs. I don't get it."

"I thought you'd be chicken," scoffed Alan. "The way I chase you to school practically every day."

"You don't chase me," said Mitchell, trying not to show that he was beginning to get angry. "I don't pay any attention, is all." He took his thumb out of his belt and grasped his handlebars until his knuckles were white.

"Not much you don't," jeered Alan. "Not much you don't pay attention."

"I do not!" Now Mitchell really was angry, and the thing that made him angriest of all was the unfairness of the situation. He knew he was right and Alan was wrong, just as he had been right and Alan had been wrong when he smashed the skate board. Chicken *was* a stupid game and smashing other people's skate boards was wrong. Alan was the one who should be unhappy, not Mitchell, but there sat Alan cocky as anything while Mitchell felt confused, not knowing what to do next.

"Well, why don't you say something?" Alan demanded.

"What do you expect me to say?" Mitchell did

not know what else to answer. He couldn't sit there on his bicycle telling Alan he was unfair, that the whole situation was unfair. "Sure, I've felt a couple of eucalyptus buds, but who cares about a couple of eucalyptus buds?"

"You do." Suddenly Alan bent over his handlebars and began to pump his bicycle. In only a fraction of a second Mitchell grasped what was happening—Alan was forcing him to play chicken, whether he wanted to or not. Mitchell knew he did not have a chance unless he got moving in a hurry. He got that other foot on the pedal and stood up and pumped as hard and as fast as he could with Alan bending over his handlebars heading straight for him.

Mitchell had another fraction of a second to make a big decision, and that fraction was all he needed. Let Alan call him chicken. He was not going to risk wrecking his three-speed bicycle for an old bully like Alan or anyone else. An instant before their bicycles would have clashed, Mitchell swerved.

"Chicken!" yelled Alan in triumph, as the front wheel of his bicycle struck a patch of gravel and he and his bicycle went sprawling on the street

with a thump and the sound of metal grating against asphalt.

Mitchell stopped to see what had happened. Alan was picking himself up slowly and stiffly. A bleeding knee showed through a tear in his jeans, and there was a scraped and muddy place on his face. The fall must have hurt and hurt a lot. Painfully Alan leaned over and lifted his bicycle upright.

Mitchell was tempted to laugh and yell, Don't you wish you were chicken? But he decided not to. Why rub it in? "Tough luck," was all he said, as he turned and started pedaling toward home. They both knew he had won, and nothing else mattered. This should put an end to the eucalpytus buds.

"I'll get you for this!" shouted Alan. "I won't let you get away with it!"

Mitchell did not look back. He did not want to see Alan standing there bleeding and shaking his fist. Boy, thought Mitchell bitterly, as he wove his way around the patches of gravel, how unfair can a fellow get? He takes a spill that was his own fault, and now he says he's going to get me for it. Well, Mitchell had learned one thing even if he had to learn it the hard way. His father and all the people who said that ignoring a bully would make him go away were wrong. At least, they were wrong if the bully was Alan Hibbler.

Mitchell wondered if the other people were wrong, too, the people who said that if you fight a bully he will back down. As Mitchell pumped hard to get a run at his steep driveway, he knew that sooner or later he was going to have to find out.

6

RAINY
SATURDAY

AMY decided being a twin was much harder on a
rainy Saturday than at any other time. Mitchell
could be so exasperating. By the time lunch was
over, she and Mitchell were in the midst of an
argument over which television program they
should watch. The argument was their second that
day, not counting the one over which had received
the shinier twenty-five cent piece for his allowance. Amy could not resist giving Mitchell a shove
when he reached over to switch the set from the
program she was watching to an old Western
movie.

"Every action has a reaction," Mitchell informed his sister as he shoved back. "It's just like the scientist told us at school. If you shove me, I have to react and shove back." Once a week a scientist talked to the fourth grades about all sorts of interesting things—molecules, air pressure, and how a satellite moved through space without a motor.

Amy was a little surprised at this application of the scientist's talk about action and reaction, which had been illustrated by a movie of a cannon reacting to firing by recoiling, but she lost no time in getting into the spirit of this new scientific development. She shoved back at Mitchell and said, "And when you shove me back, I have to react and shove you back again."

At this point Mr. Huff smiled a bit grimly, walked across the room, and turned off the television set. "When you two scuffle in front of the television set, your action causes a reaction in me. I turn off the set. No more television today."

"Aw, Dad," protested Mitchell. "That's no fair. We are the only kids in the whole school who don't get to watch TV on school nights. It isn't fair to take it away on Saturday, too."

"That's right, Dad," said Amy. "Everybody else in our room gets to watch TV on school nights."

"You poor underprivileged children," said Mr. Huff. "I can think of plenty of other things there are for you to do."

"Well, I guess I'll go practice," Amy said quickly, knowing that if her father skipped the evils-of-television lecture, he was sure to begin the you-children-don't-appreciate-your-opportunity lecture about practicing music lessons. This reaction set off a similar one in her brother. If Amy was going to practice without being told, Mitchell had to do the same or appear at a disadvantage beside his sister.

For a while the Huff household was peaceful but noisy. Amy was in her room playing Brahms' *Lullaby* on the cello, Mitchell was in his room playing *Sweet Betsy from Pike* and *Taps* on the French horn, and their father, who had always wanted to take music lessons when he was a boy and who was teaching himself to play the banjo, was in the living room plunking away at *Poor Butterfly*.

"Quite an orchestra," observed Mrs. Huff affectionately, when her family had finished practicing and put down their instruments.

"Mom, could we look at TV now?" asked Mitchell, as soon as his father had left the house to do some errands. "We wouldn't fight. Honest we wouldn't."

"We wouldn't fight anymore," said Amy earnestly. "Besides, there isn't anything to do." She knew almost at once that she had made a mistake.

"You can straighten your rooms," Mrs. Huff said promptly and walked down the hall for inspection. "Amy, look at your room—yesterday's school dress not hung up, your petticoat draped over a chair, paper and bits of cloth strewn all over the floor, your desk a jumble of crayons, jacks, doll clothes, music, crumpled paper, and old homework. And your hair things! Clips, barrettes, rubber bands, hair bands—why on earth can't you keep them all in one drawer instead of scattering them all over your room? No wonder you can never find anything. Your room is a regular mouse nest."

Mrs. Huff continued. "And Mitchell's room. Just look at it—batteries and wire tangled with coat hangers, a dried banana skin draped over the lamp, Old Maid cards and peanut shells scrambled together, little cars and marbles all over the floor. It's a wonder someone doesn't fall and break his neck. Dirty socks on the bed and probably under the bed, too, because your room smells like an old muskrat. It's a mystery to me why you can't—"

"Relax, Mom," said Mitchell. "I'll straighten it up."

Amy resisted, even though now she was appearing at a disadvantage beside her brother. "I hate picking things up. I like a messy room."

Mrs. Huff looked stern.

"Oh, all right," Amy reacted with a sigh and walked slowly down the hall to her room. Rainy Saturdays so often turned out this way. She could hear Mitchell in his room busily opening and closing drawers and making a great display of tidiness. She knew he was trying to make her look extra bad by being extra good. Amy understood this strategy, because she often behaved in exactly the same way.

Amy made a space on her desk where she quickly printed a sign, *Welcome to My Mouse Nest,* and with her crayons added a picture of a mouse peeking out from a hole with *Welcome* on a doormat.

She taped it to her bedroom door before she closed it and set about straightening her room in a leisurely way.

Amy hung up her dress and petticoat and stacked her music neatly on the bed, but somehow the faster Mitchell bustled about in the next room, the slower Amy worked. She was about to straighten her hair things when the sight of the scattered crayons on her desk tempted her to pull a sheet of paper out of a drawer and consider it a moment before she began to draw.

A lovely feeling of peace came over Amy. She drew a square box in the middle of the paper and added dials and knobs and a dozen rubbery-looking arms reaching out from the box. Each arm ended in a claw, and each claw held a picture of something she should have been picking up. One claw held a doll's dress, another a sneaker, a third a plastic hair band. Around the machine she sketched her untidy room. Then she labeled her drawing, The Handy-dandy Room Picker-upper, tacked it to her bulletin board and felt as if she had straightened her room. And someday she really would. She would discard practically everything —all the old birthday-party favors and broken crayons and outgrown toys—and have a plain bare room like a pioneer girl, a room with a bed, a chair, and one treasured old doll. Keeping a modern room neat was too much work.

Next Amy picked up her Girl Scout Handbook to see if she could apply her picture of the Handy-dandy Room Picker-upper toward a badge. She studied the list for the housekeeper badge, but as she had expected her picture was of no use. Her eye continued to travel over the requirements. She did not feel like helping her mother clean out the refrigerator, and she had already demonstrated how to use a broom, dust mop, and vacuum cleaner. She paused at, "Clean the kitchen or bathroom floor, sink, and fixtures."

Amy was suddenly full of energy. Handbook in hand, she went into the living room and asked, "Is it all right if I clean the kitchen or bathroom floor for my housekeeper badge?"

Mrs. Huff looked at Amy in astonishment. "Do my ears deceive me?" she asked. "Did you say what I thought you said?"

"Yes," said Amy smiling.

"Are you feeling all right?" asked Mrs. Huff.

"I feel fine," said Amy.

"By all means, go right ahead," said her mother. "But you had better do the kitchen floor. I scrubbed the bathroom yesterday."

Amy, who had pictured herself sweeping a bathroom, had not thought in terms of actually getting down on her hands and knees and scrubbing. She thought quickly.

"Is it all right if I ask Bonnie and Marla over to help, too?" she asked. "They're in the Agonizing Alligator Patrol, too, and are working on the housekeeper badge."

"Agonizing Alligators—what a stupid name for a patrol," remarked Mitchell on his way through the living room with an overflowing wastebasket.

Mrs. Huff ignored him and spoke to Amy. "Certainly you may ask Bonnie, but you had better tell the girls to bring their own scrubbing brushes."

"What about Mitch?" Amy asked her mother, when two invitations had been extended and accepted by telephone.

"What about him?"

"Does he have to hang around?" Amy wanted to know.

Mrs. Huff glanced at the rain slanting against

the windows. "We can hardly shove him outdoors in this weather."

"But Mom, he'll get in the way," said Amy. "You know how he is."

"Now Amy," said her mother, "Mitchell lives here, too, and there is not much for a boy to do on a rainy day."

"Well, can't he stay in his room and work on some models or something?" asked Amy. "I don't want him hanging around."

"Who wants to hang around a bunch of Agonizing Alligators?" asked Mitchell from his room and made a gagging sound.

The two girls with their Girl Scout handbooks and scrubbing brushes came splashing through the rain. "You're lucky," said Marla wistfully, when Amy had taken her raincoat. "My mother would never let me scrub our floor. Our cleaning lady might not like it."

"I had a hard time finding our scrubbing brush, because one of my little brothers had taken it to use for a hairbrush," said Bonnie, who had several young brothers and sisters.

"Amy, the scrubbing bucket is—" began Mrs. Huff, but Amy interrupted.

"I know where it is, Mom. Now you stay out of the kitchen. We know how to scrub a floor."

Mrs. Huff sat down on the couch and opened *Mastering the Art of French Cooking*. "Go right ahead," she said with a smile. "I won't say another word. Not another word. Just use plenty of elbow grease. That's all I ask."

Amy went out to the garage for the bucket, and, since there were three girls and only one bucket, she also brought back the yellow plastic bathtub she and Mitchell had used when they were babies.

"What do we do first?" asked Bonnie, pushing up the sleeves of her sweater.

"Our cleaning lady sweeps first," said Marla.

"All right, Marla, you start sweeping," said Amy, taking charge, "and we'll get the water."

The kitchen door opened, and Mitchell stuck his head in. Bonnie and Marla squealed. "Eeeee! A man!" Then they began to giggle.

"Mitchell, you're supposed to stay out of here," said Amy.

"Can a fellow help it if he's hungry?" Mitchell demanded, looking pleased with himself.

Amy broke off a banana from the bunch in the wooden bowl on the counter and handed it to her brother. "Now go away," she said. "We're busy."

"Can't I watch?"

"No, you can't." Amy shut the door in her brother's face.

She found a box of soap powder under the sink and poured some into the bucket and then into the plastic bathtub. Then, just to be sure, she added some more. Bonnie turned the water on full force, and the suds began to rise. The girls lifted the containers to the floor and swished their hands back and forth in the water until they had good thick suds. All three knelt, dipped their brushes into the suds, and began to scrub. *Swish-swish-swish* went the scrubbing brushes on the asphalt tile. Amy had never realized there could be so many drips and dribbles and scuff marks on what looked like a perfectly clean kitchen floor.

Mitchell opened the kitchen door and dangled a banana skin at arm's length into the kitchen. "What do I do with this?" he asked. All three girls stopped scrubbing. Marla and Bonnie always enjoyed watching a good fight between Amy and her brother.

"Mom!" cried Amy. "Make Mitch stay out of here!"

"Mitch, stay out of there," said Mrs. Huff.

"How's a fellow supposed to put his banana skin in the garbage if he can't go into the kitchen?" Mitchell wanted to know.

"Pest!" hissed Amy, leaving her brush on the floor and snatching the banana skin from her brother. Any other time he would drape the banana skin on his lamp or put it in his pocket. "Mom! Does *he* have to hang around interrupting all the time when we are trying to work?"

"Who's hanging around?" asked Mitchell. "Can't a fellow put a banana skin in the garbage without being accused of hanging around?"

"Mom! He's teasing!" cried Amy.

Amy could hear her mother sigh in the living room before she said, "Mitchell, can't you find something to do? Read a book or something. I brought you a book from the library yesterday."

"It isn't a good book," said Mitchell, still in the kitchen doorway. "Nothing exciting happens in the first chapter."

Amy settled the whole thing by giving Mitchell a good hard shove and shutting the door on him.

"Mom," said Mitchell from the other side of the door. "Amy pushed me."

"You children!" was all Mrs. Huff said.

The girls resumed their scrubbing. Amy and Marla shared the bathtub of suds and worked in front of the refrigerator while Bonnie tackled the linoleum near the back door. *Swish-swish-swish* went the scrubbing brushes. Rain beat down on the skylight overhead. Amy found herself growing warm from hot water and exercise, but she was enjoying the companionship of her friends. The brushes worked up a good lather, and Amy had a nice feeling of accomplishment.

"You know Bernadette, that new girl in our patrol?" asked Bonnie above the swishing.

In the living room Mitch made a gagging noise, and Amy found herself growing more and more annoyed with her brother for eavesdropping.

"You know what?" continued Bonnie to the girls. "Bernadette irons her own Scout uniform. That's why it's always sort of wrinkled."

"I'm glad I don't have to iron my own Scout uniform," said Marla, just as Amy had decided she would like to try ironing hers. "I think Bernadette is sort of funny peculiar. You know what she brought to school in her lunch one day? Cold *enchiladas* and a big dill pickle."

"I know," said Amy, who was fascinated by Bernadette. "And do you know what she said? She said the dill pickle was for *dessert*. And she sat there eating it as if it were a big piece of cake or something."

"And another time she brought some oatmeal cookies that were the most awful blue-green color," said Marla. "She said she had been experimenting with food coloring."

"And she didn't even care when everybody laughed. At least, I don't think she did," said Bonnie. "We would have to get her in our patrol at Scouts. She'll probably bring dill pickles when it's her turn to bring refreshments."

"Guess who's her refreshment partner?" said Amy. "Me!"

"Ee-yew!" cried Marla. "You poor thing!"

At that point Mitchell walked into the kitchen and picked up the telephone. The scrubbing stopped, and the girls sat back on their heels.

Amy threw down her scrubbing brush. "Mitchell Huff! You're supposed to stay out of here!"

"I just want to use the phone a minute," Mitchell said, and began to dial.

Assuming that Mitchell was making a telephone

call that might lead to his going to a friend's house, Amy allowed him to stay. The girls' conversation turned to school and the study of the California Indian, but they did not go back to scrubbing.

"Wasn't it funny when Mrs. Martin was going to show us how the Indians made acorn mush, and then all her acorns turned out to be wormy?" asked Bonnie, and the girls began to giggle.

Mitchell listened to the telephone a moment. Then he hung up without speaking. Amy looked at him suspiciously. "Who did you telephone?" she demanded.

"The time," said Mitchell with a grin.

"Mitchell Huff!" yelled Amy, annoyed with her friends for laughing as if her brother had done something unusually clever. "You didn't have to come in here. You could have looked at the clock!"

"It's more fun to phone for the time," answered Mitchell logically.

"Mitch." Mrs. Huff's tone was both warning and weary.

Amy rose from her knees and slammed the door behind her brother. The scrubbing brushes began to swish once more. Amy was so annoyed with Mitch that she began to scrub harder and faster with all her strength. She came to a raisin that someone, Mitchell no doubt, had stepped on, and she scraped it up and put it in the garbage. She scrubbed two squares of the asphalt tile at a time before she moved on to the next two squares. The three scrubbing brushes rasped companionably across the floor, when Amy heard her mother say, "Mitchell, will you *please* find something to do? Something constructive?"

The next thing Amy knew, Mitchell was opening the kitchen door again and her friends had stopped working to see what was going to happen. "Mom!" she shrieked, dropping her brush and skidding through the suds to fling herself against the door to keep her brother from entering. "Keep Mitchell out of here!"

"Mom told me to do something constructive, and I was going to—" Mitchell did not have a chance to finish.

"You don't have to be constructive in here!" shouted Amy. "Go on someplace else and be constructive. We'll never get this floor done if you keep interrupting."

Mitchell became dramatic. "Me! She blames me because she isn't getting the floor scrubbed! Here

I am trying to do something constructive while she and her friends waste their time gossiping—"

Amy shoved on the door and Mitchell shoved back, but Mitchell was stronger and Amy was standing on a soapy floor. Slowly, in spite of all she could do, the door opened. Bonnie and Marla found this struggle between brother and sister funny, but Amy did not. Then she noticed Mitchell staring over her shoulder at the floor.

"How are you going to get rid of all that lather?" Mitchell wanted to know. "You sure must have used high-suds soap."

The three girls stared at the floor. "Help! We're surrounded," said Marla, and began to giggle.

Now that she stopped to look, Amy discovered that Marla and Bonnie really were surrounded. Surrounded by a thick layer of soapy lather. Amy was standing in it, and it almost covered her sneakers.

"How are you going to get out?" asked Mitchell.

"Oh, we'll rinse it off," said Amy airily.

"How?" Mitchell, whose mind could be irritatingly logical at times, always wanted to know how things were done.

Bonnie cupped some suds in her hands and blew. A stream of bubbles came frothing out between her fingers. Amy thought she had never seen Marla laugh so hard. Then Marla snatched up a handful of suds and blew bubbles, and Bonnie laughed. One would think they had never seen soap bubbles before.

"What's so funny in there?" asked Mrs. Huff.

"Mom, you ought to see—" began Mitchell.

"No, Mom! Stay there," begged Amy. "Mitchell, go away."

"You're going to have to get those suds off the floor somehow," said Mitchell.

"You keep quiet!" yelled Amy, beginning to suspect that her floor-scrubbing party might not be a success after all. "Mom! Make Mitch leave us alone."

"You better come and look at this floor," Mitchell advised his mother.

"Oh, my goodness!" exclaimed Mrs. Huff, when she had come to inspect the kitchen floor and saw the rich layer of white lather. "And I have to start dinner in a little while."

"Too bad it isn't whipped cream," said Mitchell. "Then they could lick it up." Amy glared at her brother while Bonnie and Marla went into a gale of giggles. One would think Mitchell's remark was the funniest thing anyone had ever said. Well, they could laugh. They didn't have a twin brother.

"It will take forever to rinse it off," said Mrs. Huff. "How in the world can you get rid of it?"

"They could shovel it off if they had shovels," suggested Mitchell.

Bonnie and Marla thought this idea was hilarious. Bonnie scooped up a handful of lather and tried throwing it toward the sink, but it only drifted to the floor in bits of foam. Marla thought this sight was funny, but she could afford to laugh, Amy thought. The kitchen floor wasn't hers, and her brother wasn't standing there making fun of them. Marla didn't even have a brother, and she did not understand how a sister sometimes suffered.

"How about the dustpan?" suggested Mitchell.

"That's a great idea," agreed Bonnie. "We could scoop our way to the sink."

"I know," said Mrs. Huff. "Shirt cardboard. Mitch, go to the closet and get some of those cardboards the laundry puts in your father's shirts."

Amy could see that her brother was only too

eager to help. He ran down the hall and quickly returned with several shirt cardboards, which he handed across the lather to the girls. Bonnie used hers as a sort of snowplow and pushed a path to the sink.

"Better hurry, girls," said Mrs. Huff. "It's getting on toward dinnertime."

"I'll help," said Mitchell, who already had a shirt cardboard in his hand.

"Mom!" protested Amy.

"Better let him help," said Mrs. Huff. "It really is getting late."

"Yes, let him," said Marla and Bonnie, who looked hot and tired. "We have to be home by five o'clock."

Amy, who did not want to be left with all that lather to clean up by herself, was forced to give in. The three girls and Mitchell went to work scooping up lather into the sink and dissolving it by running cold water over it.

Mitchell was the most energetic worker of all. He enjoyed working hard when he could use his muscles. He scooped and rinsed and rubbed and helped scour the sink. Finally he spread paths of old newspapers over the floor.

"Thanks a lot, Mitch." Bonnie was much more grateful than she really needed to be.

"Mitch ought to get a housekeeper badge," said Marla, and she and Bonnie went into another gale of giggles while Mrs. Huff signed their Girl Scout handbooks to show they had completed the requirement.

"Oh, be quiet," said Mitchell, looking embarrassed but pleased.

"Thanks, Mitch," said Marla. "We never would have finished without you."

Mitchell looked even more embarrassed and even more pleased.

"Thanks." Amy could not appear completely ungrateful beside Marla and Bonnie, but the whole afternoon had been too much. That Mitch! He was always there. She never had anything all to herself. As soon as her friends had gone out the door and her mother was alone in the kitchen chopping parsley, Amy marched across a newspaper path to her side and said, "Mom, I want to have a talk with you." ·

"All right, Amy," said Mrs. Huff, laying down her knife. "What do you want to talk about?"

"Mitch," said Amy, coming directly to the

heart of the matter. "Why does he have to hang around every single time I have company? It isn't fair. It seems to me I should be able to have company once in a while without my brother hanging around. I feel deprived."

"I wouldn't say you were exactly deprived, but you do have a point," said Mrs. Huff. "You'll have to admit that today was a problem. It was raining and Mitch couldn't play outside and none of his friends were home. And he was a help."

"Yes, I know," admitted Amy. "But just the same, I wish *just once* he wouldn't hang around when I have friends over."

"All right, Amy," said Mrs. Huff. "The next time you and your friends are working on a project, I'll see to it that Mitch has something else to do."

"Thanks, Mom," said Amy gratefully. "Nobody wants a boy hanging around."

"You'd be surprised, Amy," said Mrs. Huff, as she went back to chopping parsley. "You'd be surprised."

Amy went into her room and wrote on her calendar, "Mitchell was a pest," and drew a skull and crossbones below the words.

7

MITCH AND BERNADETTE

ONE morning at breakfast Mitchell was studying some pictures of a championship boxing match in the sports section of the morning paper to see if he could pick up a few pointers in case he ever needed to use them against Alan Hibbler. A bird chirping on the pinecone outside the window made him look up from the paper, but it was his sister in her Girl Scout uniform who caught his eyes. Amy made a face at him, even though he had not done a thing to her except beat her into the bathroom a few minutes ago and then get to the comic section before she did.

"A Girl Scout is courteous," said Mitchell, who was familiar with the Girl Scout laws and did not let his sister forget them. Then he made a worse face at her.

Amy made a still worse face back at Mitchell.

Mitchell kicked his sister under the table.

Amy looked innocently out the window at a sparrow pecking at the peanut butter on the pine-cone and asked, "What is that brown bird with the striped head?" while she kicked back at Mitchell.

"It's a sparrow," said Mrs. Huff, the nearsighted birdwatcher. "Mitch, your eyes are sharper than mine. What kind of sparrow is it?"

"White-crowned," answered Mitchell, as he slid down in his chair so he could kick his sister harder.

Mr. Huff set his coffee cup on its saucer with a crash. "All right. Who started it?" he demanded.

Amy sat up straight and said nobly, "Father, I cannot tell a lie. Mitchell started it." Her nobility disappeared in a burst of giggles.

"You speak with a forked tongue," said Mitchell, glowering at his sister.

"I speak with a straight tongue," contradicted Amy. "You did kick me first."

"Yes, but—" Mitchell stopped, recognizing defeat when he saw it. If he said she started it by making a face, then she could say he started it by beating her into the bathroom.

"It doesn't matter who started it. Just stop it, both of you," ordered Mr. Huff. "And please stop talking like a pair of television Indians."

"Sure, Dad," said Amy agreeably with a triumphant look at her brother. After all, she knew and he knew that she had won.

When his parents were not looking, Mitch made a gesture of pulling back his fist as if he would like to punch his sister in the nose. Girls, he thought bitterly, as he picked up his plate and glass and carried them into the kitchen. He had had a lot of trouble with girls lately. If he barely brushed a girl's shoulder on his way to the pencil sharpener, she would raise her hand and tell the teacher he had hit her. If he denied it, at least two other girls were sure to say, "I saw him, Miss Colby, honest I did."

"Mitch, isn't this the day you pan gold?" asked Amy, and for once Mitchell was grateful to her for reminding him.

"My permission slip!" Mitchell jumped up from the table and searched through the pockets of his jacket until he found half a sheet of mimeographed paper that he had folded into a very small square several days ago. "Here, Dad. Will you sign this so I can go pan gold?"

"Pan gold?" asked Mr. Huff. "Where?"

"You see, Dad," Amy began. "All the fourth grades—"

"Amy," said Mrs. Huff, sounding a little tired. "Let Mitchell tell it."

Mitchell stopped glaring at his sister. "All the fourth grades are studying California history and —well, it tells about it on the slip. You know that new savings-and-loan company downtown? The Golden West Savings and Loan Company? They have a place in the lobby where you can pan gold. There's even a man in authentic gold-rush clothes to help. And because the fourth grades are studying California history, they get to go down and pan gold so they will really know what it was like during the gold rush. We have to write a composition afterwards, but we get to keep the gold. It's free."

"Astonishing," said Mr. Huff, studying the slip. "You mean to say there's a place in the lobby of the Golden West Savings and Loan Company where you can actually pan gold?"

"That's right," said Mitchell. "The savings-and-loan company guarantees that everyone in the class will get some gold. It's real gold, too."

"I hope it doesn't belong to the people who have deposited their money in the savings-and-loan company," said Mr. Huff.

"Of course not, Dad. The gravel with the gold in it is imported from Alaska."

"Imported gravel. Even more astonishing." Mr. Huff took his pen with the fine accountant's point out of his inside pocket and signed his name, giving his son permission to go on the field trip. "What is California coming to that it has to import gravel from Alaska?"

"Our class gets to go first, so we will probably get the most gold," said Mitchell.

At school Mitchell found that everyone in his class was just as excited about the field trip to the Golden West Savings and Loan Company as he was. Bernadette, in a somewhat rumpled Girl Scout uniform, was even wearing two matching socks for the occasion.

During social studies Miss Colby said to the class, "Since we are studying the gold-rush period of California, I think it would be nice if someone built us a model of Sutter's sawmill, where gold was discovered, to add to our collection of things to display at open house in the spring." During the period of Spanish settlement Jill Joslin, the girl whom the class called Little Miss Perfect, had built an elaborate model of a mission out of sugar cubes (it was rumored that her mother had done most of the work) and had even managed to paint it without melting the sugar. The paint made it look as if it were built of real little adobe bricks and also kept the class from eating it.

"Who would like to build us Sutter's sawmill?" asked Miss Colby.

Mitchell raised his hand along with half the class, but Bernadette Stumpf did not raise her hand. Instead she made exaggerated gestures of pointing across the aisle at Mitchell.

Miss Colby smiled. "Mitchell, how would you like to build us a sawmill?"

"I'd like to," said Mitchell. He was pleased to be chosen, but wondered if Miss Colby would have selected him if Bernadette had not pointed so wildly. When his teacher handed him a box of toothpicks to use in building the sawmill, he was a little surprised, but he stuffed it into his pocket and said nothing.

"Please bring it in by Friday when we finish our unit," said Miss Colby.

At one o'clock the class lined up, two by two, to walk down the hill to the Golden West Savings and Loan Company. Mitchell and his friend Bill Collins tried to be the last in line, so they would get to walk farthest from the teacher, but Bernadette, who had no partner, ended up there instead. For a fraction of a second Mitchell saw, or thought he saw, in Bernadette's dark eyes a look of hurt, the same sort of look he had seen in Amy's eyes when he had been invited to a birthday party and she had not. Miss Colby had to tell Sarah Smith to walk with Bernadette.

"Mitchell—ee-yew!" said Bernadette.

Mitchell glanced over his shoulder with what he hoped was a menacing look. He must have imagined that Bernadette's feelings were hurt, because she certainly did not look unhappy now.

Outside the classroom Bill Collins's mother, who had volunteered to go along on the field trip, joined the class. She brought up the rear of the line with the first-aid kit that the school board said someone must carry on every field trip. Just as if we're little kids who'll fall down and skin our knees, thought Mitchell.

"Quietly, boys and girls," said Miss Colby, as the class started across the playground.

"Forward march," said Mrs. Collins from the rear of the line. Her son Bill hunched his shoulders and looked embarrassed.

"Let's see if we can derail Mitch and Bill," said Bernadette. To derail someone meant to step on his heel so that his shoe came off.

Mitchell turned and glowered at Bernadette, who brushed her witchy hair aside and smiled at him.

"Hup, two, three," said Mrs. Collins, as the class waved to the men working on the new wing of the school and started down the hill. Bill tried to pretend he did not know his mother.

Mitchell felt the toe of Bernadette's shoe on his heel and jumped quickly to avoid having his sneaker pulled off. "You cut that out," he said to Bernadette, who, along with her partner, went into a gale of giggles.

Now Bill jumped to avoid losing his sneaker. "Don't pay any attention to them," he said to Mitchell. "They're just a couple of Girl Snouts."

"We are not," contradicted Sarah. "We're Girl Scouts."

"Hup, two, three, four. Hup, two, three, four,"

counted Mrs. Collins, who was the jolly type and did not understand how parents sometimes embarrass their children.

Down the hill marched the class. Mitchell felt Bernadette's toe on his heel again and jumped in time. "Girl Sprouts," he flung over his shoulder.

Across streets, through a park, and on down the hill marched the class, now followed by half a dozen dogs. Mitchell and Bill worked out a system to keep from having their shoes pulled off by Bernadette and Sarah. They took two or three steps and then gave a little hop, to keep the girls from matching their rhythm and stepping on their heels. Step, step, hop. Step, step, step, hop. Step, hop. By hopping at uneven intervals they kept the girls guessing.

Bernadette and Sarah found the boys' hopping extremely funny. "Just like darling little bunny rabbits," remarked Bernadette between fits of giggles.

"Hippety-hop, hippety-hop," said Sarah. "Aren't they too cute for words."

Mitchell hurled the worst name of all. "Girdle Scouts!" He only made the girls giggle more.

On down the hill and into the business district marched Miss Colby's fourth grade, with Mitchell and Bill hopping every few steps, the girls giggling, and Mrs. Collins counting from time to time. People stopped to stare. A little boy who was dribbling a chocolate ice-cream cone down the front of his shirt joined Mitchell and Bill in stepping and hopping until his mother ran after him and dragged him away.

By the time the class had reached the Golden West Savings and Loan Company, Mitchell vowed to hate all girls, with the possible exception of Amy part of the time, forever. They were nothing but giggling pests. As the class marched through the glass and stainless-steel doors Mitchell forgot to hop and Bernadette, with the awful concentration of which she was capable, stepped squarely on his heel and pulled off his sneaker.

"I'll get you for this, Bernadette," said Mitchell, jabbing her with his elbow as she went past.

"Miss Colby, Mitchell hit me," said Bernadette promptly, but in the excitement of reaching the savings-and-loan company no one paid any attention to her. She did not care because she was busy slipping through the crowd in an eely sort of way to be the first to pan gold.

Mitchell became even more annoyed. Girls, he thought bitterly, and he knelt to put his sneaker on again. They pester and then tattle if a fellow tries to get back at them.

The gold was panned in what looked like a rock pool, set on a yellow carpet, in the corner of the lobby of the savings-and-loan company. The rocks, which Mitchell soon discovered were not real rocks at all but fiber glass, were higher on one side, and a small waterfall, raised by a hidden pump, trickled down among some plastic plants into the pool. Mitchell had to wait for his turn. While he waited he looked around for the pump that worked the waterfall, but he could not find it. It must be hidden someplace inside the fake fiber-glass rocks.

When Mitchell's turn came he was handed a gold pan by a fake pioneer, a bearded student from the University, dressed in jeans, a plaid sport shirt, and a straw cowboy hat, who showed Mitchell how to scoop up some of the gravel from the bottom of the pool and swirl it around in the pan so that the water and gravel gradually spilled out, leaving the gold, which was heavy, at the bottom of the pan. Mitchell dipped and swirled and sloshed, and, sure enough, there were some glints of gold in the sand left at the bottom.

"Hey! I struck it rich!" said Mitchell, as the student picked out the flakes of gold and dropped them into a tiny glass vial of water for Mitchell to take home.

Mitchell held up his vial to the light and counted seven flakes of gold, minute but real. Someone poked him in the ribs and said, "Stick 'em up!" It was Bill, who had only five flakes of gold. One of them, however, was quite large, almost as big around as the head of a pin.

"How many did you get, Mitch?" asked Bernadette. "I got fifteen."

"Just because you pushed past everyone else and got there first," said Mitchell rudely.

"Ha-ha. Don't you wish you had?" said Bernadette, getting the last word as the class filed out through the glass doors.

Not until Thursday after school, when Mitchell was searching for a ball-point pen that worked, did he happen to run across the box of toothpicks on his desk and remember that he was supposed

to take a model of Sutter's sawmill to school the next day. Somehow the project no longer seemed as interesting as it had the day Miss Colby assigned it to him.

With his arm Mitchell cleared a space on his desk and dumped out the toothpicks. He was not sure what an old-fashioned sawmill looked like. He had seen modern mills in Northern California, but all he could remember about them were the piles of lumber and great metal cones that poured out smoke smelling of wood. He thought of the sugar-cube mission, complete with bell tower and stables, that Little Miss Perfect had built and looked at his miserable heap of toothpicks. He tried to think how a house was built, and there arose in his mind an impossible picture of concrete, studding, siding, sheetrock, plywood, tar, and gravel, none of which had been used in the construction of Sutter's sawmill.

"Drat!" said Mitchell.

"What's the matter, Mitch?" called Mrs. Huff from another room.

"Aw, nothing."

"That means something is wrong," said Amy

from her room, where Mitchell knew she was making furniture for a doll's house.

"You keep out of this," said Mitchell. He remembered watching the construction of the new savings-and-loan building where he had panned gold. Its walls were made of slabs of concrete that had been lifted into place, a type of construction known as "tilt-up." Very well, Mitchell would tilt up the walls of Sutter's sawmill.

He found a roll of Scotch tape and tore off two short strips, which he managed to lay on his desk after considerable difficulty in removing them from his fingers. Then he carefully laid toothpicks across the Scotch tape to form one wall. Placing toothpicks on sticky Scotch tape and getting them straight was difficult, but Mitchell persisted, tearing off more Scotch tape, unsticking it from his fingers, and laying rows of toothpicks on it. All the time he was thinking of the sugar-cube mission built by Little Miss Perfect, and the harder he worked the more beautiful and elaborate that mission seemed.

"Mom, do you have an old jar lid I can use?" Amy asked from the next room. "I want to put it on top of a spool to make a little round table."

Girls! thought Mitchell. They were always good at making things, especially little things. And what could he make? A skate board that Alan Hibbler wrecked.

Mitchell tried setting up the two walls of his sawmill and holding them in place while he tore off a piece of Scotch tape, which immediately twisted and stuck to itself. "Drat!" said Mitchell, louder this time. If that old Bernadette Stumpf hadn't gone and pointed to him, he probably wouldn't be all stuck up with Scotch tape.

"Mitchell, what *are* you doing?" his mother asked a second time.

"Homework," said Mitchell glumly, trying the Scotch tape once more. What kind of a sawmill was it going to be anyway, all stuck together with Scotch tape? John Sutter didn't have any Scotch tape. Mitchell managed to fasten the two walls together, only to find that one of them was crooked. He blamed Bernadette.

"Drat!" said Mitchell, and dropped a book on the floor with a satisfying bang for emphasis. If it weren't for Bernadette he could be outside riding his bicycle. Because of her he was shut up in the house with a lot of slippery little toothpicks.

Then Amy came barging into his room to see what he was doing. "Beat it," ordered Mitchell, trying too late to hide his work with his hands.

"What are you making?" his sister asked.

"Nothing that is any of your business," said Mitchell rudely.

"Come on, Mitch," pleaded Amy. "Let me help you."

"You aren't supposed to help me with my homework," he informed her. That rule was one of the most important in the Huff household. Mitchell and Amy did their own homework.

"Just tell me what you're making," begged Amy.

"Yes, Mitch," said his mother, who had joined Amy to see what was going on. "Tell us what you're making."

Mitchell glowered. "All right," he said, and raised his voice to a yell. "*I am building a stupid old Sutter's sawmill out of stupid old toothpicks!*"

"All right, all right," said Amy, backing away. "We just asked, is all. Is there any harm in asking?"

"My goodness, Mitchell," his mother said mildly. "It can't be as bad as all that."

"Did *you* ever try to build a stupid old Sutter's

sawmill out of stupid old toothpicks?" he asked ferociously.

"Well—no," admitted Mrs. Huff, "but I'm sure it can't be as difficult as you're making it seem."

"It can, too," contradicted Mitchell. Then he added darkly, thinking of all the girls who were so good at making things, "You just don't know."

"Perhaps I don't," agreed Mrs. Huff. "Do you mean this is a homework assignment?"

"Miss Colby asked me to make it and gave me the toothpicks, and I'm supposed to bring it in tomorrow," Mitchell explained. "And all because of that old Bernadette Stumpf. When Miss Colby asked who would like to build a sawmill, old Bernadette sat there pointing at me, and of course Miss Colby had to go pick on me."

"You probably had your hand raised anyway," said Amy.

Now how did she know, Mitchell wondered. Sometimes Amy seemed to understand him altogether too well, which made matters worse. Girls! They read better than he read. They were better at making things, especially little things. Old Bernadette had pointed at him, derailed his sneakers, and panned more gold. A fellow didn't have a chance.

"Anyway, Bernadette likes you," continued Amy. "That's why she picks on you."

"Oh sure," said Mitchell bitterly. "Handsome, dashing me."

"Never mind all that," said Mrs. Huff. "Let's think about Sutter's sawmill. It must have been a small wooden building, a sort of log cabin."

"Hey, that's right," said Mitchell brightening. "They had to build it out of logs, because until they built it there wasn't any mill to saw lumber."

Amy, who had edged around her brother's desk for a glimpse of his work, said, "You can't build it that way. Not with Scotch tape."

"You keep out of this," ordered Mitchell.

Amy assumed a wounded look. "I was only trying to help, is all. But if you don't want me to help, it's perfectly all right with me."

There was the trouble. Mitchell did want her to help, but he was too proud to say so.

"But Mitchell," protested Mrs. Huff, "this isn't really homework. It isn't the same as studying your spelling or working arithmetic problems. You aren't learning anything from this."

"I'm learning how hard it is to stick toothpicks together with Scotch tape," Mitchell pointed out.

"That is hardly part of the curriculum," said Mrs. Huff. "I don't see why it wouldn't be all right to let Amy help you."

"What you need is white glue," said Amy briskly, and left the room to get the plastic glue bottle.

"Go on, Mitch, let her help," whispered Mrs. Huff.

"Okay," agreed Mitchell at last. "But I have a feeling it's going to be a crummy little sawmill."

"You know, I think you're right," said Mrs. Huff with a smile.

Amy returned with the white glue and went to work in a businesslike way. She stacked the tooth-picks so they crisscrossed at the corners like a log cabin and fastened each one in place with a smid-gen of glue. With Mitchell helping, she did not take long to construct a tidy little toothpick building, with a cardboard roof, and doors and windows snipped through the toothpicks with the kitchen shears. She glued it to the lid of a shoebox so it would be easy to carry. "There," she said, looking at their work. "It's a crummy little sawmill, but I guess it is what your teacher wants."

"I guess so," agreed Mitchell, smiling for the first time since he had started working with the toothpicks. His sawmill should please Miss Colby, even though Little Miss Perfect, who had built the sugar-cube mission, and the rest of the girls would make fun of it. Well, he did not care. If he had made the sawmill alone, he would have been worried, but his sister had helped him so it was all right. Amy was one of the best makers-of-things in the fourth grade. She even got to write in starched string, the "Thanksgiving" that went over the hall bulletin board, where her class displayed mosaics made out of dried beans and peas.

Mitchell's thoughts returned to girls once more. "Did you mean it, what you said about Bernadette?" he asked his sister. "Do you really think she likes me?"

"Of course," answered Amy, as if Bernadette's liking Mitchell should be obvious to anyone. "Why else would she point at you?"

Mitchell thought the matter over. "Yeah, I see what you mean," he finally admitted. He was embarrassed to be liked by a girl like Bernadette Stumpf.

8

AMY'S FEATHERED FRIEND

ONE day in the middle of December Amy came home from school carrying a large paper bag. "Guess what, Mom!" she said, as she entered the back door into the kitchen, where her mother was mincing mushrooms with her French cookbook open beside her on the counter. "Mrs. Martin made me *piñata* chairman for the class, and I appointed Marla and Bonnie to be on the committee."

"Good," said Mrs. Huff, laying down her knife. "And just what does a *piñata* chairman do?"

"Makes a *piñata* for the Christmas party. Mrs.

Martin gave me all the things to make it with,"
answered Amy, and in her mind's eye she could
see the *piñata* her committee would make. It would
be in the shape of a bird, and when it was hung
from the ceiling of the classroom it would look
as if it were really flying. It would be so beautiful
that the class would be sorry to break it, even if
it did spill out peanuts and candy. "The committee is meeting here Saturday afternoon, and Mom,
remember your promise. You promised the next
time I had friends over to make something you
wouldn't let Mitch hang around and spoil everything."

"I remember," said Mrs. Huff with a smile.
"He can go ice skating that afternoon."

"Boy!" said Mitchell, pretending indignation
when he heard the news. "It's tough when a fellow
isn't welcome in his own house. I think I'll write
a letter to my congressman."

Amy, who knew that her brother would rather
go skating at the ice rink than almost anything
else, looked forward to a peaceful *piñata* party
without any pestering.

Saturday afternoon Amy spread newspapers on
the kitchen table and, at her mother's suggestion,

on the floor. While Marla and Bonnie took turns blowing up the balloon Mrs. Martin had supplied, Amy dumped the bag of powdered wheat-flour paste into a mixing bowl. Mrs. Huff added water and beat the paste with the wire whip she used in her French cooking until it was as smooth and free from lumps as any of the sauces she made from her French cookbook. When the balloon was larger than a basketball, the girls tied the opening with a string.

"See the balloon." Bonnie, who was good at imitating her little brothers and sisters, spoke in the flat, expressionless voice of a first grader reading from a primer. "See the big balloon."

Her imitation sent the girls off into a gale of giggles. "Look, look, Mother. See the balloon," said Amy, as if she were reciting in a first-grade reading group. She began to cut old newspapers into strips with the scissors.

"Look, Spot, look," said Bonnie. "Look at the balloon."

"Who's Spot?" asked Marla.

"Oh, you know how they always have dogs in readers," said Bonnie, as she helped Amy shred newspapers.

"Remember Penny in that reader we used to have," said Amy. "Penny lost her bunny."

The girls shrieked with laughter at the memory of poor Penny losing her bunny. Amy tried to dip a strip of newspaper into the paste only to find that the paste was now as thick as pudding. "Mom, help!" she called.

"We had better thin it out," Mrs. Huff said, when she had examined the paste. She removed half of the puddinglike stuff to a second bowl, filled both bowls with water, and once more beat out the lumps with her wire whip.

Amy dipped a strip of paper into the paste and slapped it on the dripping balloon. "Ick," she remarked.

"How gooshy," said Marla, as she dipped a strip of paper into the paste.

"Yuk," said Bonnie, going to work. "How do we make the hole so Mrs. Martin can put the candy and peanuts inside?"

"We cover the whole balloon and cut a hole after the paste dries," said Amy. "Then we break the balloon and pull it out."

The girls dipped and pasted in silence until the paste had thickened into pudding once more.

This time Amy added water to the bowls, and the girls took turns beating because they wanted to try using Mrs. Huff's wire whip.

The three continued plastering the balloon with pasty strips of paper, rolling it around as they worked so that the strips of soggy newspaper completely covered it.

While the girls worked Marla taught them a new jumping-rope rhyme:

"Charlie Chaplin went to France
To teach the ladies how to dance
And on the way he split his pants
And this is how he mended them.
Heel stitch, toe stitch, cross stitch, around stitch."

She demonstrated the footwork to go with the last line of the rhyme, and the girls' work grew careless as they pasted and jumped. Heel stitch, toe stitch, cross stitch, around stitch. They jumped heel down, toe down, ankles crossed, and turning around. Paste splattered. The girls became stickier and stickier as they dipped, dripped, and slapped paper on the balloon.

Once more Bonnie began to speak as if she were

having difficulty reading. "Look at the balloon. It is gooey." She made it even gooier by slapping on another dripping strip of newspaper.

"Look, look at the gooey balloon," recited Marla in her first-grade voice. Then she said in her natural voice, "What are some more words with *oo* sounds?"

"Look, look. The balloon is gooey. I am gooey, too," said Amy and giggled.

Marla thought of another word with an *oo* sound. "Goody. The girl is gooey. Goody, goody. Gooey, gooey girl."

"Go, gooey girl, go," was Amy's next contribution to the first-grade reader. "Goody, goody. Look at the gooey girl go."

At this point Mrs. Huff came into the kitchen. "All right, gooey girls," she said. "Don't you think you have enough paper pasted to that balloon?"

"I guess you're right," agreed Amy, as she stopped dipping and dripping to look at the big ball of soggy newspaper. "How are we going to stick wings and a tail and feathers on it when it's so wet?"

"We can't," said Marla. "We'll have to let it dry first."

"But that is going to take ages," said Bonnie. "It will probably have to dry overnight."

Amy airily waved her pasty hands. "Oh well. That just means we'll have to have another *piñata* party when it's dry. We have until Friday to finish it."

Later, when Mitchell returned from an afternoon at the ice rink, he went straight to the kitchen table. "I thought you said you were going to make a *piñata*," he said, examining the gray ball of soggy paper. "This doesn't look like any *piñata* I ever saw. It looks more like a moldy basketball."

"Oh, be quiet, Mitch." Amy was impatient with her brother. "We just have to let it dry awhile before we finish it. There is plenty of time."

"It looks pretty wet to me," said Mitchell, "but you can't blame me. I was away ice skating all afternoon."

By Monday the outer layer of newspaper was dry, but when Amy poked a bit she found that beneath the dry outside layer the *piñata* was still as soggy as it had been on Saturday.

Tuesday Mrs. Huff tried putting the damp ball of paper into an oven set at a low temperature, and soon the house began to smell of wet newspaper.

"Something cooking?" Mitchell asked brightly.

"You shut up," said Amy.

"Amy, don't be rude," said Mrs. Huff. "We don't tell people to shut up."

"Amy does," said Mitchell.

"Just my pesty little brother," said Amy.

"I'm one inch taller," Mitchell reminded his sister, "so don't call me your little brother."

"I weigh two pounds more," Amy pointed out. "Therefore, I contain more molecules than you do." Mitchell was not the only one who could apply science to argument.

Wednesday a family conference was held. The Huffs decided that cutting the hole in the *piñata* and removing the balloon would hasten the drying. When Amy tried to pierce the layers of paper with the point of the kitchen shears, she could not make a dent, but her father finally succeeded in sawing out a circle of the papier mâché with a sharp knife. When he lifted off the circle and pulled out the broken balloon, the kitchen was filled with the smell of mildewed paper.

"Pee-yew," said Mitchell. Catching Amy's eye, he added, "Don't look at me. I didn't have anything to do with your moldy old basketball."

"Oh well," said Amy, as her mother put the papier-mâché ball into the oven for further drying. "It will probably air out overnight, and tomorrow we will cover it with lots of crepe paper and maybe that will cover up some of the smell."

On Thursday afternoon after school Bonnie had an appointment with the orthodontist, so Amy had only Marla to help her cover up what the Huff family now referred to as "that moldy basketball." Mitchell had gone to Bill Collins's house after school.

"Pee-yew," was the first thing Marla said, when she caught a whiff of the big gray ball. "What happened to it?"

"It just got a little mildewed, is all," said Amy.

"Well, come on. Let's work fast," said Marla. "My mother says I have to be home before five o'clock to practice my piano before dinner."

The girls fashioned wings, a head, and a tail from shirt cardboard and fastened them in place with many strips of Scotch tape. Hurriedly they cut strips of crepe paper—red, orange, purple, and green—snipping the edges into fringe, which they hoped looked like feathers, and holding them in place with dabs of white glue. Somehow this *piñata* party was not nearly so much fun as the first one.

"Does it need feet?" asked Marla, while Amy cut a beak from a bit of cardboard and colored it yellow with crayon.

"Birds don't fly around with their feet hanging down," said Amy.

"That's good. I've got to go now or my mother will just about kill me," said Marla. "She's already mad at me, because I didn't practice before school this morning."

"There," said Amy with finality, when the beak was fastened in place. "It's done." She stepped back to look at her committee's work.

What a disappointment the gaudy bird roosting on the kitchen table was, not the least bit like the graceful *piñata* Amy had pictured in her mind's eye the day Mrs. Martin had appointed her *piñata* chairman. Its wings were lopsided, and its tail drooped from the weight of too much crepe paper. Its feathers looked unkempt, as if it were suffering from some illness peculiar to poultry. The neck was too long and placed at the wrong angle, so that it looked like the neck of a turkey rather than like that of the exotic tropical bird Amy had imagined.

And I am chairman, was Amy's first thought. Everybody will laugh. Marla began to giggle. "But it isn't supposed to be funny," said Amy.

"But it is," said Marla.

"I know," agreed Amy, and began to giggle, too.

"You can tell Mrs. Martin it's the molting season," said Marla.

The more the girls looked at the bird, the funnier it seemed. "Our feathered friend," said Amy between giggles.

Mrs. Huff came into the kitchen to see what all the laughing was about. "It certainly doesn't look like anything in *Field Guide to Western Birds*," she observed.

"It's a very rare bird," Amy told her mother. "It's so rare it's practically extinct."

"Like the whooping crane," said Mrs. Huff and laughed.

Marla glanced at the clock on the kitchen stove and snatched up her sweater. "Now my mother really will kill me."

Soon after Marla left Mitchell arrived. "Here I am, folks. Live and in color," he announced, and then his eyes rested on Amy's bird. "What is it?" he asked. "A turkey or a buzzard?"

"He is my feathered friend," said Amy, patting her bird affectionately. "He's funny-looking, but I love him, so don't you make fun of him."

Mitchell peered inside the *piñata*, sniffed it, and thumped its sides experimentally. "Boy!" he exclaimed. "That bird is as hard as concrete, and it still stinks."

"Oh!" wailed Amy. Everything seemed to go wrong. She had completely forgotten the *piñata* was supposed to be broken by a whack of a yardstick. "What am I going to do? I forgot we have to break it to get the candy and peanuts out." She turned to her mother for help.

"Nobody could break that bird with a yardstick," said Mitchell. "I bet you couldn't break it with a baseball bat. I bet you couldn't even break it with a sledgehammer."

Amy flared up. "You don't have to sound so happy about it."

"I'm just pointing out a few facts, is all," Mitchell told his sister. "Plain everyday facts."

"Mom, what am I going to do?" asked Amy. "The party is tomorrow, and there isn't time to make another *piñata*. Anyway, we used up all the paper and paste."

Mitchell had a suggestion to offer. "Maybe the class will think it's too pretty to break."

Amy dismissed this possibility. "We aren't in kindergarten. Besides, nobody could ever call it pretty. My class isn't that dumb. Mom, what am I going to do?"

"At this point there isn't much you can do," said Mrs. Huff. "Take it to school and explain what happened to Mrs. Martin. I'm sure she'll think of something. Probably she'll decide to tip it over and dump out the candy and peanuts."

When Mr. Huff came home from work, he examined Amy's feathered friend and decided it was a rare species of Paper-feathered Dingbat found only in areas of California inhabited by school children.

The next morning Amy put on her favorite dress, ate her breakfast without dawdling, and hurried through her cello practice. As she put on her jacket to go to school Mitchell came into the kitchen with his hair slicked down with water.

She turned to her mother, who was busy rinsing dishes so they would be clean enough to put in the dishwasher, and asked, "Could you drive me to school with my *piñata?* It's sort of awkward to carry."

"It isn't heavy, and Marla will help you." Mrs. Huff began to load the dishwasher. "I can't break my vow to the mothers of the neighborhood and drive you to school, they would call me a traitor and never invite me to another coffee party."

"Come on, Mom. Drive us as a special treat, because this is the day of the Christmas party," coaxed Mitchell.

"Not a chance," said their hardhearted mother cheerfully.

Amy looked at Mitchell and saw that he was thinking the same thing—Alan Hibbler. She and her brother had not mentioned Alan since the day Mitchell had come home with the broken skate board, but now they both were wondering what would happen if she met Alan Hibbler on the way to school with her *piñata.* There wouldn't be any *piñata* for the Christmas party, that's what. Amy did not know what to do. Her feathered friend with its flapping wings and drooping tail was too awkward a shape to wrap in paper.

"I'll walk to school with you, Amy," said Mitchell.

"Thanks, Mitch."

"What has come over my children?" asked Mrs. Huff, but Amy knew her mother was not waiting for an answer.

Naturally Amy did not expect her brother to walk beside her anymore than she expected him to carry her *piñata* for her. She knew that a boy will go only so far for his sister, so she was not surprised when he trailed along behind her. A brisk breeze from the North fluttered the wings and tail of Amy's feathered friend.

"Your bird looks as if it wants to fly," remarked Marla, who was waiting in front of her house. The girls walked together, the *piñata* between them, and speculated on the kind of treat their room mother would provide for the Christmas party. They decided they would prefer Hawaiian punch to apple juice and several kinds of cookies to one cupcake. They passed the eucalyptus grove and followed the winding street down the hill with Mitchell padding along behind in his sneakers looking out for Alan Hibbler.

Once past the grove of trees whose trunks were just the right thickness to hide a boy, Amy began to feel safe. She felt even safer when they passed the steep vacant lot with the clumps of greasewood, another good hiding place. Even so, she glanced over her shoulder and was pleased to see Mitchell still padding along behind, although not as close as when they had left home. He too must feel that the danger of Alan was past.

Amy and Marla began a fascinating discussion of Christmas presents they hoped to receive. Amy wanted a sewing box with a pair of really sharp scissors and some little dolls to fit the furniture she enjoyed making and books that were not educational and maybe a *few* clothes, but not things like underwear and sweaters and—

With a yell that sounded as if it came from an old Tarzan movie, Alan Hibbler leaped from an open garage near the sidewalk and landed directly in front of the girls. He was brandishing a stick. Marla screamed, but Amy was unable to move or to make a sound.

"Hey!" yelled Mitchell, and Amy heard her brother's sneakers pounding down the street.

Alan raised the stick. Amy tried to protect her *piñata* by turning around, but she was not quick enough. Alan brought his stick down *whack* squarely on Amy's feathered friend, knocking it out of her arms. The wings flapped, but they were held in place with so much Scotch tape they did not come off. *Whack!* Alan hit the *piñata* again, and again he did not even dent it.

"You cut that out!" yelled Mitchell.

Alan stopped and stared at the crepe-paper bird. "Say, what kind of *piñata* is this anyway?" he wanted to know.

"A tough *piñata*," said Amy coldly, as she rescued her feathered friend from the street. She looked at her brother standing beside her with his fists doubled up. "It's all right, Mitch. Alan can't hurt it." She wanted to laugh. Alan looked so funny standing there wondering why he hadn't broken the *piñata*.

Marla knew exactly how to behave. "When our committee makes a *piñata*," she said haughtily, "we make it to last."

"Our *piñata* is indestructible," said Amy.

"My sister's *piñata* could pass the sledgehammer test," said Mitchell.

"Stupid," said Alan. "A *piñata* is supposed to break."

Amy assumed the superior manner she some-

times used to annoy Mitchell and said, "Marla, imagine! Alan thinks a *piñata* is supposed to break." The whole thing was like a game of pretend. She and Marla were duchesses, and Alan was—Amy wasn't quite sure what he was. Somebody stupid—a stableboy or perhaps a chimney sweep.

"Well, it is!" Alan was both red in the face and indignant. "How else are you going to get the candy and junk out of it?"

Marla turned to Amy and said, as if in amazement, "Alan doesn't know how we're going to get the candy out of our *piñata*."

"And you had better get going before we hit you with it," said Mitchell. "My sister's *piñata* is so strong it could just about smash a fellow to pieces."

Alan, outnumbered even if two of the number were girls, threw down his stick in disgust. "Aw, for Pete's sake," he muttered and, turning, ran on down the hill toward school.

"I guess you told him," Amy said to Mitchell, and could see that her brother was satisfied with the way things had turned out. She was pleased, too, because she had not forgotten the broken skate board or the lunch bucket Alan had kicked in the second grade or her Brownie beanie he had snatched and thrown into the boys' bathroom when she was in the third grade.

When the three reached the school grounds, Amy and Marla carried the *piñata* to a bench that was beside the stairs leading up to the main floor of the building. Mitchell ran off to a kickball game.

"Hi, Amy," Bonnie called from the top of the steps. When Amy looked up, Bonnie held her arms out over the concrete wall that prevented Bay View pupils from falling off the landing, and called out, "Romeo, Romeo, wherefore art thou, Romeo?" A day never passed at Bay View School without at least one girl playing the balcony scene from this spot, just like Olive Oyl in an old Popeye cartoon on television.

The bell rang and quite unexpectedly Alan Hibbler's face appeared above the concrete wall, almost as if he had been crouched down waiting. Before anyone realized what was happening, Alan leaned over the railing and spat into Amy's hair. Then he turned and disappeared into the building.

The incident happened so quickly that everyone who witnessed it stood openmouthed in astonishment, not knowing what to do and unable to think of anything to say. When Amy realized what Alan had done, her eyes filled with tears of anger and humiliation.

"He's scared to spit on anyone his own size." Bernadette Stumpf, who had come in from a kick-ball game, was scornful.

"Come on, Amy," said Marla with sympathy in her voice. "Let's go to the girls' bathroom and wash the spit out of your hair."

"Yes, come on, Amy," said Bonnie, who had run down the steps. "I'll help."

Amy found herself being borne off to the tiled chill of the girls' bathroom by half-a-dozen indignant and sympathetic friends. Her eyes were full of tears, and she could scarcely see. She was so angry and so humiliated she could not speak. She *hated* Alan Hibbler. How dared he do this thing to her? Hating people was wrong, Amy knew, but at this moment, as her friends dampened paper towels under the faucets, she could not help herself. She *hated* Alan Hibbler.

The girls scrubbed the top of Amy's head with wet paper towels while they buzzed with excitement and anger.

"That old Alan Hibbler . . . thinks he can get away with anything . . . just because his father is so famous . . . who does he think he is, anyway? . . . I'm glad he isn't in *my* class . . . do you know what I heard he did one time? . . . he used to pick on Amy's brother, but now. . . ."

"Ow. Not so hard," Amy managed to protest. "There," said Marla at last, when Amy's hair was wet and rumpled by the scrubbing. "That ought to get rid of Alan's cooties."

Amy was beginning to enjoy being the center of so much concerned attention. She wiped her eyes with the back of her wrist and sniffed. "Th-thanks," she said to her friends. "Th-thanks loads."

Marla put her arm around Amy. "Come on. Let's go to class. Alan's inside the main building so it's safe. She led Amy out of the girls' bathroom toward their temporary classroom while Bonnie followed with the *piñata*.

Amy was comforted to know she had such loyal friends, but she was thinking, What about other times when my friends aren't around? She was sure to run into Alan Hibbler sometime, and what would she do then? A sentence that she had interrupted while her hair was being scrubbed came

back to her now. "He used to pick on Amy's
brother, but now. . . ." Amy did not have to
hear the rest of the words to know how the
sentence would have ended. But now he picks on
Amy.

9

CHRISTMAS VACATION

By recess Mitchell and everyone else in Miss Colby's room had heard about Alan Hibbler's spitting in Amy's hair, but as soon as their room mother appeared thoughts turned from Alan and Amy to refreshments. They were treated to pink popcorn balls, Hawaiian punch, and cookies, but Miss Colby spoiled the party for Mitchell. Just before she wished the children a merry Christmas and a happy New Year, she reminded her class that their book reports were due the week after Christmas vacation. Mitchell had a feeling that this time he could not slip through with another report on a Dr. Seuss book, because his third-grade teacher had written, "Next time try a harder book," on his last Dr. Seuss report.

"Mitch, you could lick Alan Hibbler. I know you could," said Bernadette Stumpf, when the party was over and school had been dismissed. Bernadette was wearing a long string of beads in honor of the occasion.

Mitchell jammed his fists into his pockets, hunched his shoulders, and said nothing, embarrassed because Bernadette liked him and even more embarrassed because he could not share her confidence in himself.

Halfway home Amy caught up with her brother. "Everybody was so nice to me," she said happily. "They acted as if I were—oh, you know —sort of important."

"That's good," said Mitchell, not sure he meant what he said. He was thinking about Alan Hibbler and how he would like to punch him in the nose, about how he was going to have to punch him in the nose. A boy could not let another boy get away with spitting in his sister's hair.

That night the wind changed from the North to the Southwest, and with it came the winter storms.

The Huffs were shut off from their view of the bay by storm clouds that swirled around their house like smoke. Great gusts slammed rain and wet eucalyptus leaves against the front windows and set gravel rattling across the flat tar-and-gravel roof. Eucalyptus trees, like ghosts glimpsed through the clouds, seemed to toss their branches in agony. Mitchell did what any other boy would do under the circumstances. He turned on the television set.

"Now Mitch," said Mrs. Huff almost at once. "I don't want you spending your entire Christmas vacation in front of the television set."

"But Mom," protested Mitchell, "there isn't anything to do in this kind of weather."

"You can read," said Mrs. Huff shortly.

The minute his mother began to speak about reading in that tone of voice, Mitchell balked. *He did not want to read*. He especially did not want to read when Amy was sitting there with her nose buried in a thick book.

Half an hour later Mrs. Huff snapped off the television set in the middle of one of Mitchell's favorite commercials. "Hey, Mom!" objected Mitchell.

Mrs. Huff pointed silently at several library books on the coffee table and left the room. Scowling, Mitchell shuffled through the books, looked at the pictures, and put them down again. None of the books appealed to him. One was too thin and babyish-looking. In another the children in the pictures looked too dainty. In the third, Mitchell liked the boys and girls in the illustrations because they looked lively and real, but the print in the book was too small. Mitchell went into his room to play with his little cars.

Wind and rain continued to bluster, clouds continued to swirl, and Mrs. Huff continued to turn off the television set. Mitchell and Amy popped corn, helped decorate the Christmas tree, and chopped celery and onions for the turkey stuffing. When Christmas morning finally arrived, the whole family unwrapped packages under the lighted Christmas tree until the living room was a glorious jumble of torn Christmas wrappings, ribbons, empty boxes, and excelsior.

Mitchell received a big box that contained a dry-cell battery, lots of wire, buzzers, bells, switches, sockets, and little light bulbs. He also received a real basketball, a quilted nylon jacket with a hood that could be zipped out of sight under the collar, and many smaller gifts including four model kits and two books he did not want to read.

After that television seemed less important to Mitchell, because he was busy assembling models or rigging up his buzzers, bells, and switches so that he could buzz, ring, and turn little lights on and off. From Amy's room came the sound of her new sewing machine. She was making slacks for a stuffed elephant.

Then one morning Mitchell woke up to find that his throat hurt every time he swallowed and in between swallows, too. He said, "a-a-a-a," while a flashlight was beamed down his throat, his temperature was taken, and his mother announced that he was indeed sick and that he must stay in bed. Mitchell poked at the cereal served him on a tray, nibbled at a corner of his toast, and decided he did not feel like eating anything. His mother brought him a glass of cold apple juice. Mitchell sipped his juice and dozed until lunchtime, when his mother brought him some soup. "Could I have the—" asked Mitchell, not wanting to say the word out loud.

Mrs. Huff smiled ruefully and said with a sigh,

"Oh, I suppose so," before she wheeled the television set into Mitchell's room.

Mitchell spent a feverish and languid afternoon napping and watching whatever went past on the screen—an old movie, some grown-ups playing a game, a kiddie program with a lot of old cartoons. While he poked at his supper, which Amy had carried in for him, he watched a familiar program about some fishermen catching the wily tuna fish. It was followed by the news and two cowboy programs, the best part of Mitchell's day. When the good guy fought the bad guy, Mitchell was licking Alan Hibbler.

Next Amy and Mrs. Huff joined Mitchell, and they all watched the French Chef prepare a fish soup, or *bouillabaisse*, from an assortment of fish, large and small, which involved much whacking and chopping as well as slicing and mincing with knives and cleavers.

"Fish—ugh," said Mitchell, who had no appetite and did not like fish when he did have an appetite. However, he had enjoyed watching the French Chef whack and chop.

The next morning Mitchell, at Amy's suggestion, sat up in bed long enough to wire a doorbell to his dry-cell battery so that he could summon his sister when he needed waiting on. Amy was always unusually nice to Mitchell when he was sick, almost as if she felt guilty because he was sick and was trying to make up for all the squabbles over box tops and television programs. Mitchell enjoyed lying in bed and ringing his doorbell whenever he wanted a glass of water or the television set changed to a different channel. He drank a lot of water that day just for the pleasure of ringing for Amy.

By Saturday Mitchell's temperature had dropped, and he swallowed a few bites of breakfast while he watched a nursery-school program, which was followed by an exercise program, a man interviewing some famous but boring people, and several old comedies. Amy perched on the foot of his bed to watch the comedies, and just at a funny part, where a curly-haired woman was trying on a pair of skis in her living room and was knocking over all the lamps, Mr. Huff stalked into the bedroom with the three library books, which he dropped on Mitchell's bed.

"Aw, Dad," said Mitchell, tearing his eyes away from the television set. "Those are baby books."

"Mitchell, you have to start reading sometime," his father began.

Mitchell sighed and thought, Here it comes. Mr. Huff had two lectures that he delivered from time to time. The first lecture had to do with practicing music lessons and began, "You children don't realize how fortunate you are to have music lessons." The second lecture, which was always directed at Mitchell, was about to begin.

"Mitchell, you are much too intelligent to waste so much time in front of the television set." Mr. Huff emphasized his point by switching off the set and silencing the curly-haired woman in skis. "You get nothing from it."

"Yes, I do," said Mitchell, propping his head up with his fist. "Some of it is educational."

"What?" his father challenged him. "What have you watched that is educational in the past twenty-four hours?"

"I learned all about how fishermen catch the wily tuna," Mitchell informed his father.

"That is one half hour out of an entire day of your life that has otherwise been wasted," said Mr. Huff.

"We've watched that wily tuna program lots of

times," said Amy. "It really is educational. And we watched the French Chef with Mom. Mom always watches the French Chef."

Mitchell admired Amy's strategy of bringing their mother into the discussion. "And you watch the news and football games," he reminded his father.

Mr. Huff went on, ignoring his children's side of the argument. "A day wasted when you could have been reading—"

Mitchell and Amy exchanged a glance that said, Dad is really wound up this time.

"—good books. How do you expect to get through high school and college if—"

Mitchell slumped down in bed. Years and years of having to read books stretched endlessly ahead of him. That book report. Fifth grade, sixth grade, junior high school, high school, college. . . .

"—you spend every waking minute filling your mind with—"

"Dad!" said Amy.

"—rubbish." Mr. Huff looked at Amy sitting on the foot of Mitchell's bed. "Yes, Amy?" he asked, impatient with this interruption when he was warming up to one of his favorite subjects.

"Dad," began Amy, who was sometimes inclined to be stern with her parents, "I think you are being much too hard on poor Mitch."

This time Mr. Huff did look amused. "I am?"

"Yes," said Amy earnestly, and Mitchell began to take an interest in the conversation. "He's been sick. I don't think you should pick on him when he's been sick."

Mitchell lay back on the pillow and felt thin and pale.

"I'm not picking on him. I am just pointing out—" Mr. Huff broke off in the middle of a sentence and smiled. "Maybe you're right, Amy. I'll get down off my soapbox and stop lecturing, at least for a couple of days."

"Poor little boy," said Amy sympathetically, when Mr. Huff had left the room.

"Don't you call me little," said Mitchell, who was grateful to his sister, but not that grateful.

In the afternoon the family had errands that no longer could be postponed because of the bad weather. Mrs. Huff needed groceries, Mr. Huff needed a new string for his banjo, and Amy had read all her library books as well as her Christmas books. Mitchell agreed to stay alone while his family drove out into the storm. He passed the time watching two silly game programs and an unusually boring old movie about some sailors who were trying to get a song published. He wished he had something to do.

As soon as Mitchell heard the car return and the back door open, he sat up in bed and called out, "Did you bring me something?"

"Just groceries," answered his mother.

Amy came into Mitchell's room in her raincoat and laid a library book on the bed. "I brought you something, Mitch."

Mitchell made a face, but the title caught his eye. *Wild Bill Hickok.*

"I thought you might like a book about grown-ups with shooting in it," said Amy.

"Thanks," said Mitchell, who felt he should be polite even though he did not intend to read the book. When Amy had gone to take off her raincoat, he went back to watching the movie, which was not only boring but confusing. It was full of sailors and girls, who seemed to spend their time tap-dancing or jumping into taxicabs. He finally lost interest in it entirely and lay in bed hoping for an interesting commercial, like the one about the lady who used shortening that was so light she had to chase her cake around the kitchen with a butterfly net, but even the commercials were boring. They were mostly about ladies with headaches or ladies who talked to one another about detergents.

Mitchell picked up *Wild Bill Hickok* and flicked idly through the pages while he waited for the next commercial. The book was thicker than a babyish book yet not so thick it was discouraging. The print in the book was the right size, and a sentence caught his eye. It was about shooting, and there was nothing babyish about it. It reminded him of Westerns he had seen on television.

Mitchell turned to the beginning of the book to see what it was like and suddenly thought, Hey! I can read most of these words! He read half a page and discovered that even if he skipped the words he did not know or did not want to bother to sound out, the rest of the words meant something. He finished the first page and turned to the second. Frontier scouts on horseback were a lot more interesting than tap-dancing sailors.

Mitchell read several pages before he heard his mother coming down the hall and hastily thrust the book under the bedcovers. Naturally he was

too proud to let his mother catch him reading after everyone had made such a big fuss about his not reading. He would be too embarrassed. While he drank the juice his mother had brought him, he wondered what happened next in the book, and when he was alone again he pulled it out from under the blanket and read a few more pages.

Mitchell continued to read the book, three or four pages at a time, when no one was looking, and before long he had read two chapters. And it wasn't half bad, thought Mitchell, shoving the book way down under the bedclothes.

Sunday he managed to read three chapters when no one was looking, and on Monday morning during the nursery-school program, while the children were pounding rhythm instruments and skipping around in a circle, Mitchell's foot bumped against *Wild Bill Hickok*, which had slid to the foot of the bed during the night. He dived under the covers after it, and when he had pulled it out, he began to read. He did not want to turn the television set off, because his mother might come into his room to find out if something was wrong. He continued to read, off and on, and to ignore the noise from television.

Not until the middle of the next afternoon, when Mitchell had the television set tuned to a noisy old war movie, did Mrs. Huff catch Mitchell reading the book.

"Mitchell Huff!" she cried, before he had time to shove the book under the covers. "You've been sneaking around *reading!*"

There was such joy in his mother's voice that Mitchell could not keep from grinning. "Don't beat me, Mom. Please don't beat me," he pleaded, trying not to laugh. "I didn't mean to do it. Honest I didn't."

"And you're more than halfway through the book!" marveled Mrs. Huff. "Did you begin at the beginning?"

"Of course," said Mitchell. "Where else would you begin a book?"

"Why, Mitch, I'm so proud of you." Mrs. Huff sat down on the bed and kissed her son.

"Mom, you're acting as if a miracle has happened," said Mitchell.

"It has," answered his mother, and Mitchell felt that she might be right. He was reading a book and enjoying it, and if he could read this one, he could read others, too. Maybe not as fast as Amy, but he could read, really read, and not just wade through a reader. Mitchell suddenly felt as if he had been relieved of a terrible worry. No longer would he have to dread book reports. No longer would he hope that the day his class went to the library would fall on a holiday.

"I'm going to telephone your father at the office and tell him," said Mrs. Huff. "Good news like this can't wait."

"Aw, Mom, you don't have to make such a big thing out of it," said Mitchell modestly, but just the same he was pleased when his mother insisted on telephoning his father.

"Congratulations, Mitch. I knew you could do it," said Amy, while their mother was in the kitchen. "Now you won't have to do book reports on Dr. Seuss books anymore."

Mitchell grinned and carefully marked his place in the book with a piece of paper. This was one day when he did not feel like fighting with his sister.

By the time Christmas vacation was over, the storms had subsided, Mitchell was fully recovered, and Amy, not going out of her way to be nice to him now, had squabbled with him over the Dear

Abby column in the morning paper. Mitchell got it first, and Amy said she always read Dear Abby at breakfast. Mitchell said she did not need to think she was the only member of the family who could read. Mrs. Huff settled the argument by reading Dear Abby herself to see if Abby had any advice for the mother of twins who bickered at breakfast.

Mitchell had finished *Wild Bill Hickok* and written a book report, which he had then rewritten after his mother had corrected his spelling. Mrs. Huff suggested that he should not begin his report with the sentence, "This is a book about people, places, and things," her objection being that all books were about people, places, and things. Neither did she think he should end his report by saying, "If you want to know how this book ends, read it yourself," but Mitchell liked his report the way he had written it and did not change it. He even read one of his Christmas books and decided it wasn't so bad after all.

And so, when the time came to return to school, Mitchell was feeling good. He was jogging down the hill enjoying the slippery feeling of his new quilted nylon jacket and thinking pleasant thoughts about the finished book report in his hip pocket, kickball games, the possibility of juice bars for lunch in the cafetorium when *thump!* something struck him between the shoulder blades. This time it was no little eucalyptus bud. It was something big. Mitchell turned in time to see a clump of grass, roots, and dirt flying toward him. He ducked and the grass bomb sailed over him. Mitchell was angry. So Alan Hibbler was throwing grass bombs! He did not want grass bombs muddying his new jacket. This attack was something he could not ignore.

As Mitchell watched, Alan Hibbler, who was also wearing a new quilted nylon jacket, seized two clumps of grass and pulled. The grass was strong and green and the soil was loose from the winter rains, conditions that made perfect grass bombs. "You cut that out!" yelled Mitchell, who had passed the vacant lot and was standing by a hedge.

"Make me!" Alan yelled back.

Mitchell realized he was at a disadvantage. He always seemed to be at a disadvantage when Alan was around. If he ran back up the hill to the vacant lot and pulled some grass bombs of his own, he could not hit Alan because it was almost impossible to hit anyone by throwing a grass bomb uphill. All he could do was shake his fist and yell, "You're going to be sorry!" and go jogging on down the hill to school.

Thump! Another grass bomb hit Mitchell's new jacket and bits of loose soil rolled down his neck. He grew angrier and angrier. Who did Alan think he was anyway?

Thump! Another grass bomb struck its target. Mitchell gritted his teeth. He thought of the smashed skate board and the eucalyptus buds he had worked so hard to ignore. He thought of Alan whacking Amy's *piñata*, and he thought of Alan leaning over the wall to spit in Amy's hair. By the time Mitchell reached the school grounds he had both fists doubled up with his thumbs on the outside the way his father had shown him.

Mitchell waited inside the fence, and as soon as Alan set foot on the playground, he grabbed him.

Alan was taken by surprise. "Leggo!" he shouted, trying to pull away.

Mitchell hung on with his left hand and tried to swing at Alan with his right, but Alan kept backing away and Mitchell could not get a swing at him. "I've had enough of your bullying," said Mitchell between clenched teeth. "You leave me and my sister alone."

"You just make me," said Alan with a sneer.

"Fight! Fight!" yelled the crowd that was gathering.

Mitchell threw his free arm around Alan to try to make him stand still only to find that when he hung on with both arms he could not hit. They struggled, getting nowhere like a pair of waltzing bears. Mitchell could even smell Alan's hair oil and the newness of his nylon jacket. He began to feel ridiculous. He could neither hit nor let go.

Suddenly Alan wrenched away. Mitchell, his hands free at last, put up his fists and held his chin down the way men fought on television. The trouble was, Alan was doing the same thing and he was bigger. Mitchell tried to think what would happen next if they were on television, if he were the good guy and Alan the bad guy.

"Go on, Mitch! Hit him!" yelled the boys. "Sock him good!" Girls began to squeal, and Mitchell at least had the satisfaction of knowing the whole school realized he was not afraid to stand up and fight Alan Hibbler.

Mitchell kept his head down and his shoulder up, and he and Alan edged cautiously around one another. Faces were crowding in on him, and everyone was shouting or screaming. Mitchell felt confused and his mouth was dry. With muscles tensed, he edged closer to Alan and waited for a chance to swing.

"Go on, Mitch!" he heard Bernadette Stumpf yell. "Pound him into the ground!"

Someplace in the crowd he heard Amy's voice. "Mitch! Mitch!" She sounded frightened, as if she were about to cry.

"Hit him! Hit him!" yelled the crowd, and Mitchell knew he must take a chance or Alan was going to hit him first.

Alan swung, but Mitchell saw his fist coming and ducked. The shouts grew louder, and Mitchell grew more determined. He did not want Alan to beat him up in front of the whole school. Now Mitchell gritted his teeth and swung, hitting Alan on the chest. Mitchell had a fleeting feeling of triumph. If Alan had not been well padded by his quilted jacket, that blow might have hurt.

"Atta boy, Mitch. Pound him into the ground!" screamed Bernadette, but Mitchell ducked instead. He threw up his arm in time to ward off the blow that he saw coming and prepared to swing with his right fist. Sweat stood out on his face, and he could see sweat on Alan's face, too. He wished he could stop and take off his nylon jacket. He swung, Alan stepped back, and Mitchell reached out and grabbed him by the jacket. There they were again, hanging onto one another like waltzing bears. Alan freed his right hand. Mitchell was not going to let go and give him a chance to swing. Alan pounded him on the back of his quilted jacket.

Then Mitchell felt a hand on his shoulder. "All right, boys," said Mr. Greer, the principal, who was holding Alan by the shoulder, too. "Break it up." Mitchell let go of his opponent and felt Alan release his grip.

"Aw, gee . . . that's no fair. . . ." The crowd was disappointed, and in a way so was Mitchell, because nothing had been settled. He wiped his arm across his forehead and wished he could have landed one more good hard punch on Alan.

"Now, boys," said Mr. Greer, "I want you to

remember this. Crowds would always rather watch a fight than be in one."

"But he started it, Mr. Greer," said Alan. "Honest. I was just standing there—"

"I did not!" Mitchell burst out as the bell rang. "You threw—"

"All right, boys," said Mr. Greer. "It doesn't matter who started it. It's over. Now shake hands and go into your classes, and don't let me catch you fighting again."

Mitchell did not want to shake hands with Alan, but with Mr. Greer standing over him he had to. Alan, the old apple polisher, said, "Sure, Mr. Greer," and appeared happy to shake hands.

"Aw, they didn't even get started," Mitchell heard someone complain, as the crowd surged toward their classrooms.

"Mitch, are you all right?" Amy asked anxiously when she was able to get to him.

"Sure. I'm all right." Mitchell climbed the wooden steps to his temporary classroom. He felt hot and dirty, and it seemed as if he had left home a long time ago, but he had the satisfaction of knowing he was not afraid to stand up and fight Alan Hibbler. Maybe nobody had won, but now

Alan knew Mitchell could stand up to him. Mitchell flopped into his seat. Just let Alan take off his quilted jacket and—

"Don't worry, Mitch," said Bernadette from across the aisle. "I know you could pound him into the ground."

"Thanks," muttered Mitchell, pulling his book report out of his hip pocket. He felt better than he had felt in a long time, even though the fight had not settled anything.

10

SHOWDOWN

Amy was in a difficult spot. She was avoiding Bernadette Stumpf, yet during the second week in January she and Bernadette, both members of the Agonizing Alligator Patrol of their Scout troop, were supposed to provide refreshments for the troop meeting. And how was Amy going to get together with a girl she was avoiding?

Amy could fight with her own brother, give him a push or a shove, but she did not want him to fight with anyone who might hurt him, and she did not like the way Bernadette cheered him on, jumping up and down and yelling, "Come on,

Mitch! Pound him into the ground!" He wasn't Bernadette's brother. And anyway, wondered Amy, what kind of refreshments would a girl like Bernadette want to take to Scouts? Dill pickles? Purple cookies?

But if Amy did not know what to do, Bernadette did. She simply telephoned Amy one evening and said, "What are we going to do about those refreshments?"

"We could take butterscotch brownies," suggested Amy, who liked to bake and who felt that brownies were appropriate because all the girls had been Brownies before they flew up to Scouts.

"I was thinking of chocolate-covered doughnuts," said Bernadette. "I like frosting."

The girls compromised on frosted chocolate cupcakes. Amy planned to bake her half in her own kitchen, but Bernadette changed this arrangement. "We can bake them at my house," said Bernadette, taking charge. "My mother won't care. Besides, we have such a big family we have lots of muffin tins."

"But you have all those brothers," said Amy, thinking of her own brother. "Won't they hang around sticking their fingers in the frosting?"

Bernadette considered. "One has a paper route and one is going to the University and gets home late and one has this girl and doesn't hang around the house much and one has a violin lesson on Monday after school and the other is always over at a friend's house developing his muscles. Yes, it's safe."

So reluctantly Amy agreed to go to Bernadette's house after school on Monday to bake cupcakes. She did, however, ask her mother to provide cake and frosting mixes as well as fluted paper cups for three dozen cupcakes, because she was doubtful of Bernadette's ability to follow a recipe.

"You poor thing," said Marla, when she heard what Amy was planning to do. "Be sure and tell us what her house is like."

"You might have fun," said Bonnie, trying to look on the cheerful side.

On Monday after school Amy walked home with Bernadette to a big old brown-shingled house in a canyon under some redwood trees. There was a go-cart in the garage, the body of an old car on the driveway, and a pair of hockey sticks beside the front door, which had been deeply scratched by a dog asking to be let in. Bernadette fished a key out of the mailbox and unlocked the door.

The outside of the house should have prepared Amy for the inside, but when she stepped into the living room she had to remind herself she must be polite and not act surprised. The dusty upright piano was old and scarred, the couch and chairs were shabby, and the carpet was covered with dog hair. There was a coffee table at the side of the room, and on it rested the internal parts of a hi-fi—turntable, tubes, and wires. The speakers were suspended from the ceiling in two corners of the room. There was no television set but phonograph records were everywhere, in a cabinet, under the coffee table, on the couch. Amy had never seen so many phonograph records.

"My mother is a terrible housekeeper," said Bernadette matter-of-factly.

Amy did not feel that she would be polite to agree out loud. Besides, she liked Bernadette's living room. It had a used, comfortable look, and its windows framed a view of the bay through the redwood trees.

"She says she doesn't need neatness," continued Bernadette, not in the least apologetic.

"Doesn't need neatness?" echoed Amy, who

had never heard of such a thing. "I thought all grown-ups . . . needed neatness." Certainly her own mother did, although she was not as bad as Marla's mother about being neat.

"Not my mother," said Bernadette, as she tossed her jacket onto a chair. "She says she has more important things to do than try to keep a house full of boys neat. She says it's a losing battle."

Amy was curious to know what Bernadette's mother had to do that was more important than neatness. "Isn't your mother home?" she asked.

"She'll be home after a while," said Bernadette. "She has a late class on Monday."

"Where does she teach?" asked Amy, as she followed Bernadette into the kitchen, where she was not surprised to see breakfast dishes still sitting on an old-fashioned round table.

"Oh, my mother doesn't teach," said Bernadette. "She goes to school."

"Goes to school?"

"Yes. Monday is her long day, because she has a chemistry lab." Bernadette found a large mixing bowl in a cupboard and made space for it on the counter among the open cereal boxes and milky glasses. "She goes to the University and hopes to graduate this year if she can get through chemistry. I think she will. Two of my brothers are good in chemistry, and they are helping her."

Amy, who had never heard of children helping their parents with homework, was full of more questions than she thought polite to ask about this topsy-turvy household. She finally selected the most important. "How come your mother is going to school?"

Bernadette turned on the oven, rummaged about in a cupboard for muffin tins, and all the while she chattered. "Mother got married before she finished college and had all us kids, and now she says with so many of us to educate she's going to have to go to work to help Daddy out. She wants to finish college so she can get a really interesting job. Besides, she says housework is boring, and we are all old enough to take some responsibility around here."

Amy did not know what she had expected at the Stumpfs' house, but she had not expected a student mother. She had often heard mothers say they thought they would take a few courses at the University to keep their minds from getting rusty, and sometimes they even attended lectures, but

Bernadette's mother was the first one Amy had heard of who actually went so far as to do homework.

When Bernadette opened the refrigerator to take out the eggs, a dog began to scratch and whine at the back door, and she let a dignified old collie into the kitchen. Two small gray cats shot in through the door at the same time. "Hello, Buckley, old fellow," she said, hugging the dog while the meowing cats wove themselves around her ankles.

Amy felt she could no longer stand there staring, so she got out the package of paper cups and set them into the muffin tins while Bernadette scooped a double handful of dry dog food out of a bag under the sink and dropped it into a dish beside the back door. Buckley began to eat and so did the cats, which crouched beneath his chin. The kitchen was filled with the sounds of many teeth gnawing and grinding.

While this activity was going on, Amy noticed what appeared to be two tennis balls inside a sock suspended from the light fixture in the middle of the kitchen. "Is that a sock?" she asked, not quite believing what she saw.

"Oh, *that*," said Bernadette lightly. "My brother, the one who is always developing his muscles, uses it for a punching bag. We're going to get him a real one for his birthday and put it in the garage. It's an awful nuisance when we're all trying to eat breakfast and pack lunches to have him standing there punching away at an old sock."

Amy could see how a punching bag in the kitchen might be a nuisance. She stood by, feeling useless, while Bernadette dumped the boxes of cake mix into the bowl, added eggs, and measured water. For a wild moment Amy half expected Bernadette to imitate a book character, Pippi Longstocking, and beat the batter with a bath brush, but Bernadette produced a proper wooden spoon and began to beat with all her usual energy. By now Amy plainly realized that Bernadette was a girl who knew her way around a kitchen. "Isn't there something I can do to help?" she asked.

"You can fill the paper cups with batter," suggested Bernadette. "I want to get the meat loaf started."

"Meat loaf?"

"Sure," said Bernadette briskly, as she removed what looked to Amy like an enormous quantity of hamburger from the refrigerator. Buckley whimpered, and the two gray cats stood on their hind legs and clung to her skirt with their fore claws. "Yow," said Bernadette, skillfully balancing the bundle of hamburger on one hand and unhooking the cats' claws with the other. She tossed some meat into the animals' dish as she talked. "I make meat loaf every Monday because Mother gets home so late. Meat loaf, baked potatoes, and squash. They all go into the oven at the same time." She paused to consult a recipe for meat loaf on an oatmeal carton.

"I can cook some things, but not meat loaf." Amy was trying to get an equal amount of batter into each paper cup and thinking, Wait till I tell Marla that Bernadette cooks meat loaf all by herself.

"Anyone who can read can cook," said Bernadette a bit scornfully.

Amy wondered if they had needed to use mixes after all. She was beginning to like Bernadette and so would Marla when she got to know her better. Marla would love Bernadette's house, everything was so messy.

When the cupcakes came out of the oven to

cool and the meat loaf went in, Amy prepared the instant frosting while Bernadette hacked up a large piece of squash with a cleaver. "If you keep both hands on the cleaver, you can't cut yourself," she exclaimed, noticing Amy's look of alarm.

The cupcakes were cool enough to frost when Mrs. Stumpf came through the back door. "Hi, girls," she said, and dropped a load of books and her raincoat onto a kitchen chair. Amy noticed she was dressed like a college girl in an olive-green sweater and skirt and flat-heeled shoes. Her straight hair, streaked with gray, was pulled back from her face and held in place by a wooden clasp.

"Mom, this is Amy Huff," said Bernadette. "Mitchell's twin sister."

"Hello, Amy. I'm glad you could come over. We've heard a lot of nice things about the Huff twins."

"Thank you," said Amy shyly.

Mrs. Stumpf set a coffeepot on the stove to re-heat. While she waited for the coffee to heat she set about stacking the breakfast dishes as if this chore were the usual thing to do at five o'clock in the afternoon.

"Mother says it's inefficient to wash dishes more

than once a day," Bernadette explained. "Why go through all the motions three times when once is enough?"

"That's right," agreed Mrs. Stumpf. "And a waste of soap and hot water as well as motion."

Amy thought this opinion over while she spread frosting on the cupcakes with a knife.

Mrs. Stumpf poured herself a cup of coffee and sat down at the kitchen table. "It feels good to sit down after standing in that lab all afternoon," she said, as both cats tried to jump on her lap. She held one and stroked the other with her foot after she had kicked off her shoe.

"Was chemistry lab hard?" asked Bernadette sympathetically.

"It was dreadful," said Mrs. Stumpf. "I'm beginning to think that even with the boys helping me I won't be able to get through."

"Yes, you will," said Bernadette. "You keep trying and you'll make it."

Amy almost laughed. She had heard this bit of encouragement often, but in her own house the grown-ups encouraged the children.

When the cupcakes were frosted and carefully packed in two shoe boxes, Mrs. Stumpf drove

Amy and one box of cupcakes home in a Volks-
wagen bus. "You must come over to our house
again," she told Amy, when she had stopped the
bus at the foot of the Huffs' driveway.

"I'd like to and thank you for the nice time and
the ride home," Amy answered politely before
she ran up her driveway. She couldn't wait to
telephone Marla.

Mitchell was in the kitchen looking in the oven
and lifting the lids of the pans on the stove to see
what they were going to have for dinner. "What
was it like at Bernadette's house?" he wanted to
know, as soon as Amy came through the back
door.

"Nice." Amy set her box of cupcakes on the
kitchen table. "Nice and messy. Bernadette says
her mother doesn't need neatness."

"No kidding?" Mitchell was as surprised as Amy
had been. "Are you going to tell Mom?"

"Maybe sometime." Amy went into her room
and tossed her jacket on her bed before she picked
up her ball-point pen, the one that wrote in three
colors, and wrote, in red beneath the date on her
calendar, "Today I made a friend." Then she cir-
cled the date with blue and green scallops.

The next morning Amy, walking with Marla, carried her box of cupcakes to school and set it along with her school books on the asphalt beside the fence while the girls ran off to look for Bonnie. The next thing she knew, Marla was grabbing her arm.

"Look!" Marla gasped, pointing.

Amy looked and what she saw infuriated her. Alan Hibbler was leaning against the fence, and he was *eating one of her chocolate cupcakes!* He could not do this. She needed every one of those cupcakes for Scouts. Who did he think he was anyway? He had no right. . . .

"You stop that!" Amy yelled across the playground, as she ran toward Alan. She stopped in front of him, planted her hands on her hips, and said fiercely, "You can't eat my cupcakes. I need them for Scouts this afternoon."

Alan popped the last bite of cupcake into his mouth and licked a bit of frosting from his fingers before he said, "Hm-m. Not bad."

Amy was almost but not quite speechless with rage. "Didn't you hear me? I said *you can't eat my cupcakes.*"

"And who is going to stop me?" asked Alan. "Your brother?"

Amy was outraged by Alan's sneering manner, but Marla shouted, "He wasn't afraid to fight you once."

Amy glanced around the playground and caught a glimpse of Mitchell's back at the other end of the school yard, where he was playing fielder in a kickball game. She did not want him to get into another fight.

"Next time sprinkle some nuts on the frosting," said Alan. "It needs that little touch."

"You—you're *despicable*," Amy sputtered, and wished Mr. Greer or the yard teacher would appear. The temporary buildings made the crowded playground difficult to supervise.

Alan laughed, calmly leaned over, and helped himself to another cupcake from Amy's shoe box. This sight was too much for Amy, who darted over and tried to snatch the cupcake from his hand, only to have it crumble and leave her fingers sticky with frosting.

"*Oh!*"—Now Amy was really speechless.

Alan leaned against the fence and laughed.

Amy almost wished Mitchell were there. Maybe between them they could. . . .

"Is that old bully eating our cupcakes?" Bernadette had appeared beside Amy with her own shoe box in her hands.

Amy nodded, tears of rage in her eyes.

"You big bully!" yelled Bernadette. "Just because your father is so famous you think you can get away with anything!"

Alan stopped laughing. "You leave my father out of this!" he yelled back, every bit as angry as the girls.

"Well, it's true!" taunted Bernadette. "Just because he gets his picture in *Life* magazine you think you can do anything you want!"

"You sure do!" shouted Marla.

Alan's face turned red as he faced the three angry girls, who were now joined by others. A ball came bouncing across the playground, and Amy automatically stuck her foot out to stop it.

"You must think you're smart because your father is," shouted Marla. "Well, you're not. You're just a big bully!"

Mitchell came running to retrieve the ball and stopped short when he saw what was happening.

"Hey, Huff! Bring the ball back!" called someone from the kickball game. When Mitchell did not move, there was nothing for the players to do but join him to see what was going on.

Alan looked angry enough to explode. "You shut up!" he yelled at the girls. "I'm sick of hearing about my father!"

"Alan Hibbler's father! Alan Hibbler's father! Yah! Yah!" Marla yelled.

Bernadette joined in. "Judson Hibbler! Yah! Yah! Judson Hibbler!"

"You shut up, or I'll wreck the whole box of cupcakes!"

"Alan Hibbler's father! Alan Hibbler's father," chanted Marla and Bonnie.

"No, you won't wreck my box of cupcakes!" said Amy ferociously. She was so mad at Alan she wanted to pound him as hard as she could with both her fists.

"Yes, I will!" shouted Alan. "I'll wreck your whole box. H-o-w-l. *Whole* box!"

"Go on, let's see you!" yelled some of the boys.

But h-o-w-l spells howl, not whole, thought Amy, startled. The same thought must have been going through the minds of her friends, because they all began to laugh at the same time.

"He's going to wreck the howl box," shrieked Bernadette and doubled up with laughter. "The h-o-w-l box, *howl* box!"

The sudden laughter took Alan by surprise. He hesitated, and then looked even redder and angrier than before. Amy stopped laughing. She was still furious with Alan, more furious than she had ever been with Mitchell, but she could not laugh at him because she suddenly understood that he had the same trouble with words as Mitchell. What if Mitchell were standing there with half the school laughing at him? And the situation must be a lot worse for Alan, having a famous father the way he did. Maybe his father was the reason he picked on people and tried to act big all the time.

Angry as she was, Amy began to feel sorry for Alan. She glanced at Mitchell and saw that he was not laughing either. He was standing there with the ball in his hands and a funny look on his face. She wondered if Alan had to read aloud to his mother the way Mitchell did before he started reading for himself, and she thought how embarrassed he must be to stumble over baby words

while such a famous and distinguished father listened.

"Howl box! H-o-w-l spells whole!" Everyone thought Alan's mistake was funny except Alan and Amy and Mitchell. Alan raised his foot and was about to bring it down on the lid of Amy's shoe box full of cupcakes when Bernadette thrust her own box of cupcakes into Amy's hands, rushed at Alan, expertly hooked her toe behind the ankle of the foot he was standing on, and, with a good hard shove, pushed him to the ground. Obviously Bernadette was used to handling bigger boys. With one knee on Alan's chest and her fist raised, she said, "Whose box of cupcakes are you going to wreck?"

Alan said nothing while Marla darted in and rescued Amy's cupcakes, which were dangerously close to Alan's feet.

"Go on, Bernadette. Sock him!" yelled some of the boys, but most of the boys in the crowd were laughing.

Amy looked at Mitchell and saw that he was thinking the same thing she was, almost as if the two of them were sharing a secret without having to use words. Poor Alan. How shameful to let a girl get him down.

"Aw, come on get up, for Pete's sake." Alan was painfully embarrassed, too embarrassed even to struggle.

"Whose box of cupcakes are you going to wreck?" repeated Bernadette. The bell rang, but no one moved.

Amy forgot about Mitchell's skate board and the time Alan leaned over the railing to spit in her hair. She only knew she could stand Alan's shame no longer. What if Mitchell were down there on that asphalt? "Let him up, Bernadette," she pleaded. "It's all right. Let him up."

Reluctantly Bernadette took her knee off Alan's chest. Trying to avoid the eyes of the crowd, Alan got to his feet just as Mr. Greer made his way through the boys and girls who had witnessed Alan's defeat.

"What's going on?" demanded the principal.

Amy made up her mind right then she was not going to tell.

"Nothing," muttered Alan, unable to raise his eyes above Mr. Greer's shoelaces.

"Alan was wrecking the cupcakes Amy baked for Scouts," explained Marla.

"Is that right?" Mr. Greer asked of Amy.

Amy felt shy and embarrassed to have the principal speak to her in front of everyone, but she spoke up. "Sort of," she had to admit. But she added, "It's all right, Mr. Greer. He just ate one. We have enough cupcakes." And perhaps they did, because one or two girls were nearly always absent from Scouts.

"Are you sure of that?" asked Mr. Greer.

"Yes, Mr. Greer," answered Amy, and was aware that Alan managed to lift his eyes from Mr. Greer's shoelaces long enough to give her a look that, although it could not be called grateful, was one of surprise and not of anger.

"All right, Amy, if you say so," said Mr. Greer, and then he turned to Alan. "Just the same, you had better come along to my office. I think it's time we had a talk."

"Yes, sir." Alan, who looked smaller than usual beside the principal, followed Mr. Greer toward the main building of the school while the rest of the crowd started toward their classrooms.

Now the girls turned on Amy. "What did you do that for?" demanded Marla.

"You know he's just a big bully," said Bonnie.

"I know he is but . . . oh, I don't know. Thanks anyway for rescuing the cupcakes." Amy took the box from Marla. She could not explain to her friends why she had behaved as she did. None of her friends had a twin brother who made embarrassing mistakes in reading and spelling. Her friends were all in fast reading groups and never spelled *they* with an *a* instead of an *e*, because the word sounded as if it should have an *a* in it. Her friends thought Alan was funny when he spelled *whole* as if it were *howl*, but *whole* really did sound as if it should be spelled h-o-w-l. Alan wasn't stupid. He had made a natural mistake. Couldn't they see?

Amy let her friends go on ahead and walked beside Mitchell. "Bernadette sure took care of Alan," he remarked, but he was not gloating, just stating a fact.

"I guess she's had a lot of practice with all those brothers," said Amy.

"Old Alan won't dare bully me or anyone else

after letting a girl get him down," said Mitchell. "He was pretty embarrassed, poor guy."

Amy agreed. "After that he won't even dare pick on a Brownie and throw her beanie into the boys' bathroom," but before she had finished the sentence, Mitchell was gone, bounding across the asphalt as if he had springs in his sneakers and not a care in the world. Amy watched him and as he took the steps to his temporary classroom in one leap, she thought, I'm glad there are two of us, one me and one Mitchell.

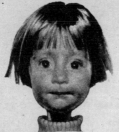